NO ONE WOULD NOTICE IF HE RAN AWAY...

Jim crept forward, invisible in the deep shadows, and stood, hardly breathing, just inside the gate. He heard the carpet woman laughing quietly, and at that moment he took his chance. He slinked himself like a cat into a thin, small shape, and glided out through the gate. He tiptoed along the other side of the railings and stood with his breath in his mouth till a cart rumbled past. He darted out behind it and ran alongside it until he was well past the workhouse, till his breath was bursting out of him. At last he fell, weak and panting, into the black well of a side alley.

He was free.

"Doherty has imagined Jim's story with bleak realism. Readers will be drawn as much by the social conditions as by Jim's picaresque adventures."

—*Booklist*

OTHER PUFFIN BOOKS YOU MAY ENJOY

STREET CHILD

CHILD

Berlie Doherty

PUFFIN BOOKS

For Hilda Cotterill

With thanks to the children of Lynne Healy's class at Dobcroft
Junior School in Sheffield, who helped me with their advice and
enthusiasm, and to Priscilla Hodgson, Deborah Walters, Mike
Higginbottom, the Barnardo Library, Dickens House, the
Ellesmere Port Boat Museum, and Sheffield Libraries, who all
helped me with their knowledge.

PUFFIN BOOKS
Published by the Penguin Group
Penguin Books USA Inc., 375 Hudson Street, New York, New York 10014, U.S.A.
Penguin Books Ltd, 27 Wrights Lane, London W8 5TZ, England
Penguin Books Australia Ltd, Ringwood, Victoria, Australia
Penguin Books Canada Ltd, 10 Alcorn Avenue, Toronto, Ontario, Canada M4V 3B2
Penguin Books (N.Z.) Ltd, 182-190 Wairau Road, Auckland 10, New Zealand

Penguin Books Ltd, Registered Offices: Harmondsworth, Middlesex, England

First published in Great Britain by Hamish Hamilton Ltd, 1993
First published in the United States of America by Orchard Books, 1994
Reprinted by arrangement with Orchard Books, New York
Published in Puffin Books, 1996

1 3 5 7 9 10 8 6 4 2

LIBRARY OF CONGRESS CATALOGING-IN-PUBLICATION DATA
Doherty, Berlie.
Street child / Berlie Doherty.
p. cm.
"First published in 1993 by Hamish Hamilton Ltd."—verso t.p.
Summary: A fictional account of the experiences of Jim Jarvis, a young orphan
who escapes the workhouse in 1860's London and survives brutal treatment
and desperate circumstances until he is taken in by Dr. Bernardo,
founder of a school for the city's "ragged" children.
ISBN 0-14-037936-3 (pbk.)
[1. Orphans—Fiction. 2. Homeless persons—Fiction.
3. London (England)—Fiction.] I. Title.
PZ7.D6947St 1996] [Fic]—dc20 96-11041 CIP AC

Printed in the United States of America

Contents

Jim Jarvis. Want to know who that is? It's me! That's my name. Only thing I've got is my name. And I've give it away to this man. Barnie, his name is, or something like that. He told me once, only I forgot it, see, and I don't like to ask him again. "Mister," I call him—to his face, that is. But there's a little space in my head where his name is Barnie.

He keeps asking me things. He wants to know my story, that's what he tells me. "My story, mister? What d'you want to know that for? Ain't much of a story, mine ain't." And he looks at me, all quiet.

"It is, Jim," he says. "It's a very special story. It changed my life, child, meeting you."

Funny that, ain't it? Because he changed my life, Barnie did.

I can't believe my luck, and that's a fact. Here I am with food in my belly, and good hot food at that, and plenty more where that came from, he says. I'm wearing clothes that smell nice and that don't have no holes in, neither. And I'm in this room where there's a great big fire burning, and plenty more logs to put on it so it won't just die off. There's just me and him. The other boys are upstairs in their hammocks, all cozy in the big room we sleep in. And downstairs there's just me and him, special.

I want to laugh. I'm so full of something that I want to

1

laugh out loud, and I stuff my fist in my mouth to stop myself.

Barnie gives me that look, all quiet. "Just tell me your story."

My story! Well. I creep back to the fire for this. I hug my knees. I close my eyes to shut out the way the flames dance about and the way his shadow and mine climb up and down the walls. I shut out the sound of the fire sniffing like a dog at a rat hole. And I think I can hear someone talking, very softly. It's a woman's voice, talking to a child. I think she's talking to me.

"Mister," I says, just whispering so's I don't chase the voice away, "can I tell you about my ma?"

1

The Shilling Pie

Jim Jarvis hopped about on the edge of the road, his feet blue with cold. Passing carriages flung muddy snow up into his face and his eyes, and the swaying horses slithered and skidded as they were whipped on by their drivers. At last Jim saw his chance and made a dash for it through the traffic. The little shops in the dark street all glowed yellow with their hanging lamps, and Jim dodged from one light to the next until he came to the shop he was looking for. It was the meat-pudding shop. Hungry boys and skinny dogs hovered around the doorway, watching for scraps. Jim pushed past them, his coin as hot as a piece of coal in his fist. He could hear his stomach gurgling as the rich smell of hot gravy met him.

Mrs. Hodder was trying to sweep the soggy floor and sprinkle new straw down when Jim ran in.

"You can run right out again," she shouted to him. "If I'm not sick of little boys today!"

"But I've come to buy a pudding!" Jim told her. He

danced up and down, opening and closing his fist so that his coin winked at her like an eye.

She prized it out of his hand and bit it. "Where did you find this, little shrimp?" she asked him. "And stop your dancing! You're making me rock like a ship at sea!"

Jim hopped onto a dry patch of straw. "Ma's purse. And she said there won't be no more, because that's the last shilling we got, and I know that's true because I emptied it for her. So make it a good one, Mrs. Hodder. Make it big, and lots of gravy!"

He ran home with the pie clutched to his chest, warming him through its cloth wrapping. Some of the boys outside the shop tried to chase him, but he soon lost them in the dark alleys, his heart thudding with fear that they would catch him and steal the pie.

At last he came to his home, in a house so full of families that he sometimes wondered how the floors and walls didn't come tumbling down with the weight and the noise of them all. He ran up the stairs and burst into the room his own family lived in. He was panting with triumph and excitement.

"I've got the pie! I've got the pie!" he sang out.

"Sh!" His sister Emily was kneeling on the floor, and she turned around to him sharply. "Ma's asleep, Jim."

Lizzie jumped up and ran to him, pulling him over toward the fire so that they could spread out the pudding cloth on the hearth. They broke off chunks of pastry and dipped them into the brimming gravy.

"What about Ma?" asked Lizzie.

"She won't want it," Emily said. "She never eats."

Lizzie pulled Jim's hand back as he was reaching out for another chunk. "But the gravy might do her good," she suggested. "Just a little taste. Stop shoveling it down so fast, Jim. Let Ma have a bit."

She turned around to her mother's pile of bedding and pulled back the ragged cover.

"Ma," she whispered. "Try a bit. It's lovely!"

She held a piece of gravy-soaked piecrust to her lips, but her mother shook her head and turned over, huddling her rug around her.

"I'll have it!" said Jim, but Lizzie put it on the corner of her mother's bed rags.

"She might feel like it later," she said. "The smell might tempt her."

"I told you," said Emily. "She don't want food no more. That's what she said."

Jim paused for a moment in his eating, his hand resting over his portion of pie in case his sisters snatched it away from him. "What's the matter with Ma?" he asked.

"Nothing's the matter," said Emily. She chucked a log onto the fire, watching how the flames curled themselves around it.

"She's tired is all," Lizzie prompted her. "She just wants to sleep, don't she?"

"But she's been asleep all day," Jim said. "And yesterday. And the day before."

"Just eat your pie," said Emily. "You heard what she said. There's no more shillings in that purse, so don't expect no more pies after this one."

"She'll get better soon," Lizzie said. "And then she'll be able to go back to work. There's lots of jobs for cooks. We'll soon be out of this place. That's what she told me, Jim."

"Will we go back to our cottage?" Jim asked.

Lizzie shook her head. "You know we can't go there, Jim. We had to move out when Father died."

"Eat your pie," said Emily. "She wants us to enjoy it."

But the pie had grown cold before the children finished it. They pulled their rag pile close to the hearth and curled up together, Jim between Emily and Lizzie. In all the rooms of the house they could hear people muttering and yawning and scratching. Outside in the street, dogs were howling, and carriage wheels rumbled on the slushy roads.

Jim lay awake. He could hear how his mother's breath rattled in her throat, and he knew by the way she tossed and turned that she wasn't asleep. He could tell by the way his sisters lay taut and still on each side of him that they were awake, too, listening through the night to its noises, longing for day to come.

2

The Stick Man

They must have slept in the end. The next thing Jim heard was a stamping of heavy feet on the stairs and the rapping of a cane on the floor outside their room.

"The Stick Man!" whispered Emily.

Before the children could sit up, the door was flung open, and in strode the owner of the house, stamping snow off his boots. He swung off his cape, scattering snowflakes around the room, and as he shook it into the hearth, the white embers spat.

"I did knock," Mr. Spink barked. "But when lie-abeds don't answer, then lie-abeds must be got up."

Emily and Lizzie scrambled to their feet at once. Jim would have crawled under the covers, but his sisters hauled him up between them. The children stood in a limp row in front of their mother.

Mr. Spink pushed the damp, yellowy strings of his hair behind his ears and peered over their heads at her. His breath came in little wheezing gasps.

"Is she dead?"

"No, sir, she ain't dead," said Emily, fright catching at her throat.

"Sick, then?"

"No, sir, she ain't sick, neither," Emily said.

Jim looked at her in surprise. It seemed to him that his mother was very sick, and had been for days.

"Then if she ain't dead nor sick, what's she doing down there? Lying under the covers like a grand lady with nothing to do! Hiding, is she? Counting all her money?" Mr. Spink pushed the children out of the way and lifted up the rag pile with his cane.

The children's mother had her eyes closed, though the lids fluttered slightly. In the daylight Jim could see how pale she was. He felt for Lizzie's hand.

"Leave her, sir. She's tired out, she's been working that hard," Emily said. "She'll be off out to work again soon."

Jim could tell by the way her voice shook how afraid she was, and how brave she was to talk back to Mr. Spink like that.

"Well, if she's been working, she can pay her rent, and we'll all be happy. Up you get, woman!" With the silver tip of his stick, he lifted the rags clean away from her.

Lizzie knelt down and helped her mother to sit up.

"Where's your money, Mrs. Jarvis?" Mr. Spink thrust his cane under his arm and stood with his hands in his pockets, jingling the loose coins there like little bells, as if they made sweet music to his ears. He saw the purse bag on the floor and peered down at it. He leaned down toward Jim, who backed away from his wheezy breath.

"I'm an old man, and I don't bend. Pick up that purse for me, sonny."

Jim bent down and picked it up. He held it out at arm's length for Mr. Spink to take, but the man rolled his eyes at him.

"Is it empty, sonny? Empty?" he said, as if he couldn't believe it. He saw the pie cloth in the hearth, with the crumbs of pastry that the children had left, and the stain of gravy on it. He started back as if the sight of it amazed him, and glared around at them all.

"Did you eat pie last night?"

The girls were silent.

"Did you, sonny?"

"Yes," Jim whispered.

"Was it a lovely meat pie, all hot and full of gravy?"

"I don't know." Jim's throat was as tight as if he still had a piece of pastry stuck there, refusing to be swallowed. He looked at Emily, who had her lips set in a firm line, and at Lizzie, who was sitting now with her head bent so that her hair dangled across her face, hiding it. He looked at his mother, white and quiet.

"I bought it," he burst out. "It was Ma's last shilling, but I bought the pie."

He heard Emily give out a little sigh beside him.

Mr. Spink nodded. "No money." He nodded again, and for a moment Jim thought he'd done the right thing to tell him that the pie had cost him Ma's last shilling.

Mr. Spink put out his sweaty hand and took the purse from Jim. He pushed his fingers into it as though it were a glove puppet, and then he dropped it onto the floor and jabbed at it with his stick. He took out his silk handkerchief and flapped it open, wiped his hair and his face with it, and then had a good blow.

"Oh dear," he said. He blew his nose long and hard. Jim stole a glance at Emily, but she wouldn't look at him. "No money, no rent." Mr. Spink blew his nose again. "No rent, no room, Mrs. Jarvis."

"We've nowhere else to go," said Jim's mother, so quietly that Mr. Spink had to stop blowing his nose and bend toward her to listen.

"Ma," said Jim. "Couldn't we go back to the cottage? I liked it better there."

Mr. Spink gave a shout of laughter, and for a moment again Jim thought he'd said the right thing.

"Your cottage! When you came crawling to me twelve months ago, you was glad of this place, make no mistake about it. But if you like a cottage better, find yourself a father, and let him pay for one. Can you do that?"

Jim shook his head. He swallowed hard. His throat filled up again.

"We're quite happy here," Jim's mother said. "Give us a little longer, and we'll pay our rent. The girls can help me."

Mr. Spink flapped his handkerchief again and stuffed it into his pocket.

"I've made up my mind, Mrs. Jarvis. I've a family wants to move in here tonight. There's eight of them— don't they deserve a home, now? And what's more— they can pay me for it!"

He swung his steaming cape back over his shoulders and strode out of the room, and they listened in silence to the sound of his cane tap-tap-tapping on the floor outside the next room.

Jim watched with a cold dread as his sisters moved slowly around the room, gathering up their belongings. They had no furniture, though they had seemed to have plenty when they piled it high on the cart the day they left their cottage. But it had all been sold, piece by piece, and what hadn't been good enough to sell had been broken up and used as firewood.

"Get your horse, Jim," Emily said, indicating the wooden horse that Jim's father had carved for him two Christmases ago. "And Lizzie's boots. You might as well have them. They're too small for Lizzie now."

He picked them up. The boots were too big for him to wear yet, but he folded his arms over them and stuck the wooden horse between them. The children stood by the doorway clutching their bundles, while Mrs. Jarvis tied her bonnet and fastened her shawl around herself. She moved slowly and quietly, as if all her thoughts were wrapped up deep inside her and she was afraid of breaking them. At last she was ready. She looked around the bare room. The snow had stopped, and sunlight came watery through the window.

"Ma . . . ," said Emily.

Mrs. Jarvis looked down at her daughter. She was pale and strained. "I'm coming," she said.

"But where can we go?"

"I'll find us a home," her mother said. "Don't worry."

3

Rosie and Judd

As the morning passed, it seemed to Jim that his mother was growing weaker. She had started off with such hope, and now it seemed to be draining away from her. As he trailed behind, he could see how she kept stumbling as she walked. She often needed to be helped along by Emily and Lizzie as she led the children away from the slums where they had lived for the past year. They trudged down street after street until they came to a much quieter part of town, where the houses were big and stately. Here she leaned against some railings to rest. Jim and his sisters gathered around her, not knowing where they were or what was going to happen next. Emily sat down by her mother, anxious for her.

"Now you've got to be good," Mrs. Jarvis said to them. "I'm going to take you to the house where I used to work, only you must be good. Promise me now?"

"Ma! 'Course we'll be good," Emily said.

Mrs. Jarvis nodded. "Yes. You're always good," she said. "That's one thing I did right, anyway."

In the window behind them a finch sang in a tiny cage. It only had room to hop from the floor of its cage to a little perch and down again—hop, hop, hop, up and down.

"Listen to that bird," said Jim.

"They only sing when they're on their own," Emily told him. "He's singing for a friend."

"Poor little thing," said Lizzie. "Trapped in a cage."

"We'd better go on," their mother said. "I'm going to take you to see the only friend I've got in the world. Rosie, she's called. You've heard me talk about Rosie at the big house?"

The children nodded. It was a long time since their mother had worked in his lordship's kitchen, but she still had stories to tell them about it.

"And if Rosie can't help us," she sighed, "nobody can." Emily helped her up again, and they moved slowly on, pausing as the carriages swept past them.

When they reached the big house at last, Mrs. Jarvis was exhausted and sat down on the steps to rest again. The children gazed up at the tall building.

"Is this where we're going to live?" asked Lizzie.

"It's too grand for us, Lizzie!" said Emily. Even though she was only ten, she knew that families like theirs didn't end up in houses like these.

Jim's eyes were fixed on something he could see on the top steps, just by the front door. It was an iron boot scraper, and it was in the shape of a dog's head. The huge snapping mouth of the dog was wide open, so people could scrape the mud off their boots in its teeth. "I'd never put my foot in there," he said. "Not even with Lizzie's boots on, I wouldn't. It'd come snarling down at me and bite my toes right off."

When their mother was rested, she picked up her bundle again and led the children down some steps to the basement of the house. She sank against the door, all strength gone.

"Be good," she murmured to them. She lifted the knocker.

They heard rapid footsteps coming. Mrs. Jarvis quickly bent down and kissed both the girls on the tops of their heads.

"God bless you both," she said.

Emily looked up at her, suddenly afraid. She was about to ask her mother what was happening, when the door was opened by a large, floury woman in a white pinafore. She had the sleeves of her dress rolled up so that her arms bulged out of them. Her hands and wrists were covered in dough, and as she flung up her arms in greeting, Jim could see that her elbows were red and powdery.

"Annie Jarvis!" the woman gasped. "I never thought to see you again!" She hugged her, covering her with bits of dough. "You ain't come looking for work, have you, after all this time? Judd's going spare, she is, looking for a new cook. She's got me at it, and my dough's like a boulder—you could build cathedrals out of it, and they wouldn't ever fall down! She'll soon put me back on serving upstairs!"

While she was talking, she hauled Mrs. Jarvis and the children into the kitchen and set stools for them around the stove, balancing herself on a high chair and scooping up more flour. She pushed aside the big mixing bowl and sat with her elbows on the table, beaming across at them; and then her smile changed. She reached over to Mrs. Jarvis and put her hand on her forehead.

"Hot!" Her voice was soft with concern. "You're so hot, Annie, and white as snow." She looked at the children, and at the bundles of clothes and belongings that they were still clutching. "You've been turned out, haven't you?"

Mrs. Jarvis nodded.

"You got anywhere?"

"No."

"And you're not fit for work. You know that? There's no work left in you, Annie Jarvis."

A bell jangled over the door, and Rosie jumped up and ran to the stove.

"Lord, that's for the coffees, and I ain't done them. Anyone comes down, you duck under the table quick, mind," she said to the children. The bell rang again.

"All right, all right," she shouted. "His lordship can wait five minutes, can't he, while I talk to my friend here?"

She glanced at Mrs. Jarvis again, her face puckered

in frowns. "My sister, good as. No, he can't wait. His lordship waits for nothing."

As she was talking, she was ladling coffee and milk into jugs and setting them on a tray. She rubbed her floury hands on the pinafore, took it off, and changed into a clean one. As a quick afterthought, she poured some of the coffee into a cup and edged it across the table toward Mrs. Jarvis.

"Go on," she urged. "Take it for all the good bread you've baked for him." She ran to the door with her tray rattling in her hand and paused to make a face at the bell as it jangled again. "There's only one home left to you now, Annie. It's the House, ain't it, heaven help you. The workhouse!"

As soon as Rosie had left the kitchen and gone upstairs with her tray, Jim slid off his stool and ran to his mother. She sipped at her coffee, holding the cup with both hands.

"We ain't going to the workhouse, Ma?" Emily asked her.

The children had heard terrifying stories about workhouses. Old people spoke of them with fear and hate, as if they were worse than hell on earth. They'd heard that people who went there sometimes had to stay for the rest of their lives. People died in there. Some people slept out in the streets and the fields rather than go to the workhouse. The two girls sat in silent dread on each side of their mother.

"Help Rosie out with her bread, Emily," Mrs. Jarvis suggested, her voice steady now, and stronger. "It'd be a good turn that she'd appreciate, and his lordship would, too!"

Emily did as she was told. She washed her hands in the jug of water on the side and then poured some of the frothing yeast into the bowl of flour.

A few minutes later Rosie came down. She put her finger to her lips and pointed up the stairs. "I've asked Judd to come!" she mouthed.

There was the rustle of a long skirt on the stairs, and the housekeeper came in, stern and brisk. Jim tried to slide under the table, but she stopped him with her booted foot.

She came straight to Mrs. Jarvis and stood with her hands on her hips, looking down at her. "Rosie tells me you're in a bad way, Annie Jarvis," she said. "And I must say, you look it."

"I haven't come to make trouble, Judd," Mrs. Jarvis said. "And I'm sorry if I've interrupted the work. I've only come to say good-bye to you and Rosie, because you've always been so kind to me."

"If we've been kind to you, it's because you've always done your work well, and that's what matters," Judd sniffed. She looked over Emily's shoulder as the girl dolloped her dough onto the table and pushed her hands into it to knead it. Rosie dodged behind her, her hands clasped together, her face anxious. The way the three women watched her in silence, it was as if Emily were performing some kind of magic and they were afraid to break the spell.

"Can cook, can you?" Judd asked Emily at last.

"She can cook as well as me," said Jim's mother. "And she can scrub the floor for you, and run errands. She can sleep on the kitchen floor and take up no room."

"She wouldn't need paying," Rosie said. "She'd be a saving, Judd."

Emily flattened and rolled the dough with the heel of her hand, stretching it out and folding it over time and time again, listening with every nerve in her body to what the women behind her were saying.

"But I couldn't do anything for the other girl," Judd said.

"Judd, I've a sister who's cook at Sunbury. She might give her a chance," Rosie said. She stood on the tips of her toes like a little girl, her hands clasped behind her back and her eyes pleading. "If you just let little Lizzie sleep down here with Emily till Sunday, I can walk her over to Moll's then."

"I don't want to know they're here, Rosie. If his lordship finds out, it's every one of us for the workhouse. You know that, don't you? I don't know they're here, these girls."

Judd swept out, her straight back and her firm stride telling them that she had never seen these girls in the kitchen. They listened to the swing of the door and for the clicking of her boots on the stairs to die away.

"It's the best I can do to help you, Annie," Rosie said. "I can't do no more."

"It's more than I expected," Mrs. Jarvis said. "At least you've saved my girls from that place."

She stood up unsteadily. "We'd better go," she said to Jim. "It's not fair to Rosie if we stay here any longer."

"I'll leave you alone to say your good-byes, then," said Rosie. She touched her friend quickly on the shoulder and went into the scullery, her face set in hurt, hard lines. They could hear her in there, banging pots around as if she were setting up an orchestra.

Emily said nothing at all, and that was because she couldn't. Her throat was tight with a band of pain. She couldn't even look at her mother or at Jim, but hugged them quickly and went to sit down at the table, her head in her hands. Lizzie tried to follow her example, but as soon as Mrs. Jarvis had put her hand on the door that led up to the street, she burst out, "Take us with you, Ma. Don't leave us here!"

"I can't," her mother said. She didn't turn around to her. "Bless you. I can't. This is best for you. God bless you, both of you."

She took Jim's hand and bundled him quickly out of the door. Jim didn't dare look at her. He didn't dare listen to the sounds that she was making now that they were out into the day. He held his face up to the sky and let the snowflakes flutter against his cheeks to cool him. He had no idea what was going to happen to him or his mother, or whether he would ever see Emily and Lizzie again. He was more frightened than he had ever been in his life.

4

The Workhouse

Jim and his mother walked for most of that day but made very slow progress. They rested a bit near a statue of a man on a horse, and after a very short distance they had to stop again for Mrs. Jarvis to scoop water from a fountain. And on they went, trudging and stopping, trudging and stopping, until Jim's mother could go no further. She put her arms around Jim and pressed her head down onto his shoulder.

"God help you, Jim," she said.

It seemed to Jim that she was simply tired then of walking and that she had decided to go to sleep, there on the pavement. He squatted down beside her, glad of a chance to rest, feeling dizzy and tired himself, and was aware of a worry of voices around him, like flies buzzing. Someone shook him, and he opened his eyes.

"Where d'you live?" a voice said.

Jim sat up. Already it was growing dark. There were

people around him, and some were kneeling by his mother, trying to lift her. "We used to live in a cottage," said Jim. "We had a cow and some hens."

"Where d'you live now?" It was a different voice, a bit sharper than the last one. Jim tried to remember the name of the street where they had rented a room in Mr. Spink's big house, and couldn't. He couldn't understand why his mother didn't wake up. He looked around for his bundle and saw that his wooden horse had gone. He clutched Lizzie's old boots.

"You haven't got nowhere?" the same voice asked.

Jim shook his head. Someone was doing something to his mother—rubbing her hands, it looked like, dabbing her face with her shawl. "Get them to the workhouse," someone said. "There's nothing we can do for her."

"I'm not taking them there," another voice said. "Prison would be better than there. Tell them we caught the boy stealing, and let them put them both in prison."

"Someone stole my horse," Jim heard himself saying. He couldn't keep his voice steady. "I didn't steal anything."

"Give him his horse back," someone else said. "It's all he's got, ain't it? A pair of boots what's too big for him, and a wooden horse. Give it back." There was a burst of laughter, and some children broke away from the group and ran off.

The next minute there was a shouting from the far end of the street, and the people who had been crouching around Jim and his mother stood up and moved away. He heard other voices and looked up to see two policemen.

"Get up!" one of the policemen ordered. Jim struggled to his feet. "And you! Get up!" the other one said to Jim's mother. She lay quite still.

The first policeman waved his hand, and a boy with a cart ran up. Between them they lifted Jim's mother onto it. Jim watched, afraid.

"Take 'em to the workhouse," the policeman said. "Let them die in there, if they have to." The boy began to run then, head down, skidding on the snowy road, weaving the cart in and out of the carriages, and Jim ran anxiously behind.

They came at last to a massive stone building with iron railings around it. Weary people slouched there, begging for food. The boy stopped the cart outside the huge iron gates and pulled the bell. Jim could hear it clanging in the distance. At last the gates were pulled open by a porter, who glared out at them, his lantern held up high.

"Two more for you," said the boy. "One for the infirmary, one for school."

The porter led them into a yard. There on the steps on each side of the main door stood a man and woman, as straight and thin and waxy-faced as a pair of church candles, staring down at them. The boy held out his hand and was given a small coin, and the master and matron bent down and lifted Jim's mother off the cart and carried her into the house. The boy pushed his cart out, and the porter clanged the gates shut.

The matron poked her head sharply around the door.

"Get in!" she told Jim, and pulled him through. "You come and get scrubbed and cropped."

The doors groaned shut. They were in a long corridor, gloomy with candle shadow. In front of them a man trudged with Jim's mother across his shoulder.

"Where's Ma going?" Jim asked, his voice echoing against the tiles like the whimpering of a tiny, scared animal.

"Where's she going? Infirmary, that's where she's going. Wants feeding and medicine, no doubt, and nothing to buy it with neither."

"Can I go with her?"

"Go with her? A big strong boy like you? You cannot! If you're good, Mr. Sissons might let you see her tomorrow. Good, mind! Know what good means?" The matron closed her ice-cold hand over his and bent down toward him, her black bonnet crinkling. Her teeth were as black and twisted as the railings in the yard.

She pulled Jim along the corridor and into a huge green room, where boys sat in silence, staring at one another and at the bare walls. They all watched Jim as he was led through the room and out into another yard.

"Joseph!" the matron called, and a bent man shuffled after her. His head hung below his shoulders like a stumpy bird's. He helped her strip off Jim's clothes and sluice him down with icy water from the pump. Then Jim was pulled into rough, itchy clothes, and his hair was tugged and jagged at with a blunt pair of scissors until his scalp felt as if it had been torn into pieces.

He let it all happen to him. He was too frightened to resist. All he wanted was to be with his mother.

He was led back into a huge hall and told to join the queue of silent boys there. They stood with their heads bowed and with bowls in their hands. There were hundreds and hundreds of people in the room, all sitting at long tables, all eating in silence. The only sounds were the scraping of the knives and forks and the noise of chewing and gulping. All the benches faced the same way. Mr. Sissons stood on a raised box at the end of the room, watching the boys who were still waiting for their food.

Jim was given a ladle of broth and a corner of bread.

"I don't want anything," he started to say, and was pushed along in the queue. He followed the boy in front of him and he sat down on one of the benches. He glanced around him, trying to catch someone's eye, but none of the boys looked at him. They all ate with their heads bowed down, staring into their bowls. The boy next to him sneaked his hand across and grabbed Jim's bread. Jim ate his broth in silence.

After the meal, the man with the hanging head gave Jim a blanket and showed him a room full of shelves and long boxes where all the boys slept. He pointed to the box Jim was to sleep in. Jim climbed into it and found that he only just had enough room to turn over in it, small though he was. He tied Lizzie's boots to his wrists in case anyone tried to steal them. The dormitory door was locked, and the boys lay in darkness.

During the night an old woman prowled up and down the room with a candle in her hand, holding it up to each boy's face as she passed. Jim could hear boys crying, stifling their sobs as she came and went—little puffs of sound that were hardly there at all. He lay with his eyes closed, the candlelight burning red against his eyelids as she approached and stopped by him. He could hear her snuffly breath and the creak of her boots. He hardly dared to breathe.

He lay awake all night, thinking about Emily and Lizzie and worrying about his mother. He longed to see her again. If she was better, maybe she could ask Mr. Sissons to let them go.

As soon as it was morning, the door was unlocked. Old Marion's place was taken by the bent man. He shouted at the boys to queue up in the yard for their wash.

"I've already broken the ice for you," he told them. "So no thinking you can dodge it."

Jim ran after him. The man was so stooped that the top half of his body was curved down like a walking stick, and when Jim spoke to him he swung his head around to look at the boy's feet.

"Please, sir—," Jim said.

"I'm not *sir*," the man said. "I'm only doing my turn, like the rest of them. I'm only Joseph, not *sir*." He swung his head away from Jim's feet and spat on the ground. "I hate *sir*, same as you."

"Please, Joseph, tell me where the infirmary is."

"Why should I tell you that?" Joseph asked, his eyes fixed on Jim's feet again.

"Because my ma's there, and I've been good," Jim said. "Mrs. Sissons said if I was good I could go and see Ma in the infirmary today."

"So you was the boy as came in last night, and your ma was brought on a cart?"

"Yes," said Jim. "Please tell me where the infirmary is."

Joseph made a little chewing noise. "Well, it's upstairs," he said at last. He rubbed his nose with the back of his hand and tilted his head sideways, squinting around at Jim. "Only the message I was given by Mrs. Sissons is, don't bother taking the boy up there, because his ma—" He stopped and shook his head and chewed again. "Your ma's dead, son."

5

Behind Bars

J im forced his fists deep into his pockets and turned
his face away. There were boys all around him,
shuffling out to the cold yard, and they blurred into
smudges of gray. He screwed up his eyes against the
terrible blinding white of the sky. He wouldn't cry here.
His lungs were bursting and he thought he would never
be able to gasp for air again, but he couldn't cry here.
The only person he wanted to be with was Rosie. She
would know what to do. She would tell Emily and
Lizzie. But there was no chance of being with Rosie.

"I want to go home," he said.

Joseph swung his head and spat. "Home?" he said.
"What d'you mean, home? What's this, if it ain't home?"

So, Jim thought, this is my home now, this huge
building with iron bars at the windows and iron railings
outside. His parents must be Mr. and Mrs. Sissons, as
thin and waxy-pale as candles. And if they were his
parents, then his brothers and sisters were the sham-
bling, skinny boys who slept and sobbed in the same

room as him, and the scrawny girls who seemed to have forgotten how to smile.

"Can't I see her, all the same?"

Joseph shook his head. "She was took into the dead-house in the night and put on the paupers' cart before light, son. Speedy dispatch, paupers get. No money for bells nor nothing like that, eh?"

Jim went dumbly from room to room as he was told: from the sleeping boxes to the yard, the refectory, the yard, and back to his box. . . . It was like a slow dance, and the steps were always the same, repeated day after day.

Morning started with the six o'clock bell, when all the boys had to wash under the pump. Joseph watched them, swinging his head from side to side and bending his neck around like a hunched bird of prey. He kept flapping his arms across his bent chest to beat the cold away.

"Get yerselfs washed quick, boys," he said. "Afore the wevver bites me bones off."

Across the yard from the pump was the asylum. Mad people were locked up there. They wailed and shrieked for hours on end. They stretched their hands out through the bars of their prison. "Give us some bread, boy!" they begged. "Let me out! Let me out!"

"Don't take no notice of them," a woolly-headed boy whispered to Jim one day. "They're mad. They're animals."

Jim was shocked. He stared again at the men and women and children who were all squashed up together. Their cage was too small to hold them all. Their wailings echoed around the yard all the time. "Animals, animals," Jim said to himself, trying to drive their noises out of his head. He looked away from them, pretending they weren't there.

"No, they're not animals, Jim," Joseph told him. "They're people, they are. People, Jim. My ma's in there."

There was a shed at the other end of the yard. Boys gazed out at them through a small barred window. Their white faces were even more frightening than the wailings of the mad people. Joseph sidled over to Jim that first morning and swung his arm across the boy's shoulder, bringing his head around to mutter down Jim's ear, "Now, them's the boys what tried to run away. They catch 'em and beat 'em and stick 'em in there till they're good. Remember that."

After the cold wash in the yard, Jim had to help clean it out with brooms twice as tall as he was. The boys had to sweep the yard till the ground was bare and clean, even if hundreds of leaves had fallen in the night and come drifting over the high walls.

At breakfast the boys queued up with their bowls in their hands for bread and tea. The bread was meant to last for every meal, but if Jim tried to save it, he soon had it stolen by one of the older boys. He learned to gulp his food down as quickly as they did: boiled meat at dinnertime, cheese at night, all swallowed rapidly and in silence.

Sometimes Mr. Sissons read to them while they were

eating—always Bible stories—and his whistly voice
would glide around the echoing room over the clatter
of knives and forks. Jim never listened to him. All he
wanted to do was to think about his mother and Emily
and Lizzie.

But every now and then Mr. Sissons stopped reading
and lowered his book. He stared around the room, his
eyes like round, glassy balls and his fingers cracking
together. Jim stopped eating, afraid that he had done
something wrong. He sat with his spoon held somewhere between his mouth and his bowl, until the boy
next to him nudged him into action again. Mr. Sissons
put down his book and jumped off his dais. He came
gliding down the aisles between the long tables like a
thin black shadow. Jim could just see him out of the
corner of his eye. He didn't dare for the life of him
look up.

The master lunged out at one of the boys at random,
pulling him away from his bench by the back of his
collar and sending his bowl flying and the contents
spattering across the faces and clothes of the other
boys.

"Misbehaving, were you?" he said, his voice as dry as
a hissing swan's. "Eating like a pig? Get to the trough,
animal!" And the boy crouched on his hands and knees
in front of a pig's trough that was always there and had
to eat his food from that, without a fork or spoon.
Sometimes there were half a dozen people troughing,
usually just for Mr. Sissons's amusement.

Please don't let it be me. Please don't let it be me,

Jim said deep inside himself as Mr. Sissons glided past and the air turned as cold as ice around him.

Jim had no idea how long he had been at the workhouse when he began to think of trying to escape. At first it seemed an impossible idea, as impossible as making the pump in the yard turn into a tree and blaze out with leaves and blossoms. He remembered the runaway boys locked up in the shed in the yard for everyone to see. Even so, he had to try. One day, he promised himself, he would go. He would watch out every moment, sharp as a bird, for a chance to fly. And when he did, he would never be caught.

He was almost too afraid to allow himself to think about it, in case Mr. Sissons pounced inside his thoughts and strapped him to a chair and beat him as he beat other reckless boys.

It was only at night that he let himself imagine escaping, as though he was opening up a box of secret treasure in the dark. Old Marion crept and wheezed her candle-path around the room where the boys lay in their boxes pretending to sleep, and Jim let his thoughts wander then. He would escape. He would run and run through the streets of London until he was a long, long way from the workhouse. He would find a place that was safe. And he would call it home.

6

Tip

At first Jim couldn't tell one boy from another. They all had the same sallow, thin faces and dark sunken eyes, and they all wore the same scratchy gray clothes and caps. They had their hair cropped and combed in exactly the same way, except for the boy who had spoken to him in the yard. His hair had a wild way of its own. Jim found himself following this boy around because he was the only one he could recognize, but it was a long time before he spoke to him. It was a long time before Jim felt like talking to anyone. He was numb, and wrapped up inside himself, but one morning in the schoolroom Tip spoke to him and became the nearest thing to a friend that Jim could ever hope to have.

The schoolroom where the boys spent every morning was a long, dim room with candles set into every other desk. The little window had been painted over so that they couldn't look out. There was a fireplace at one end with sheets steaming around it. Old women sometimes wandered in to see to the sheets, putting wet ones up and taking down the dry ones to be packed off back to the big houses. These were the washerwomen, and this was their workhouse job: washing the clothes of the rich. The women would sit by the fire from time to time, mumbling to one another in low drones during the lessons, sometimes cackling out remarks to the boys or shouting out the wrong answers to the deaf old schoolmaster's questions.

There were four big arches across the ceiling with letters on them, and Mr. Barrack would begin every day by pointing at the arches and then by asking one of the boys to read out the words on them. "God is good, God is holy, God is just, God is love," the women would chant out before the boys had a chance, sometimes in the wrong order just for fun, and they would nudge one another and screech with laughter.

One morning when it was Tip's turn to answer the question, he turned to the women and held out his hand for them to speak. They shook their heads and pursed their lips, shaking with silent laughter, and Tip, taken by surprise, laughed out loud. Mr. Barrack shook him by the back of his jacket, half lifting him off the floor.

"There's nothing to laugh at here," he shouted.

"No, sir, there ain't," agreed Tip, and was given another shaking. The women loved this.

For most of the rest of the morning, Mr. Barrack read out loud to the boys, pacing up and down the room as he spoke, so the candle flames fluttered in his wake and his black shadow danced on the walls. Curled in his

hand was the end of a knotted rope, which he swung
as he walked, striking it across a desk from time to time
to make the boys jump awake. Every now and then he
stopped and pointed at a boy, who had to stand up and
recite the sentence he'd just heard. If he got it wrong,
Mr. Barrack swung the knotted end of the rope across
the boy's hand.

As a change from reading out loud, Mr. Barrack
would shout at one of the boys to fetch him his shabby
old copy of *Dr. Mavor's Spelling Primer*. He would pounce
on any one of them. "Spell *chimbley*!" he would shout,
swinging his rope in readiness.

One morning the boys were given chalks and slates
to use. A visitor had brought them in as a present. They
sat on the desks through the morning, and the boys all
watched them lovingly, longing to have a go.

"Now you can write!" Mr. Barrack told them at last,
easing himself onto the high stool of his desk and
grunting with the effort. Tip put up his hand.

"Please, sir. What should we write?"

"Speak up!"

"What should we write?" Tip roared.

Mr. Barrack roared back, "What should you write?
The Lord's Prayer, if you please!"

Jim risked a look around at the boys as they bent to
their task, their breath smoking from them into the
cold air. He put his elbows on the desk and his head
in his hands. He was bleak inside himself, lonely and
bewildered and afraid.

Beside him Tip squeaked his chalk across his slate,

scratching out scrawly shapes. His tongue poked out between his lips as he worked. He glanced sideways at Jim.

"Why aincha writing?" he whispered.

" 'Cos I can't," Jim whispered back. "I never knew how to write."

"Cor, it's easy!" Tip's eyebrows shot up and disappeared into the tangle of his hair. "Just wiggle your chalk across the slate like this." His chalk scraped and labored. "There!" He leaned back in triumph and blew chalk dust off his slate. He showed it to Jim.

"That's good," Jim agreed. "What does it say, though?"

Tip's amazed eyebrows shot up into his hair again. "I don't know! I can't read!"

Jim spluttered into his hands, and Mr. Barrack jerked awake. He hobbled down the aisle toward Jim.

"Did you laugh then?"

Jim felt as if he had frozen into his seat. His lips stuck together as if ice had formed between them.

"No, he didn't. It was me." Tip jumped up as the schoolmaster swung his rope in readiness and swished it down across the boy's outstretched hand. The women folding up the sheets by the fire cackled. The other boys sat in total silence while this was happening, staring straight in front of them, their arms folded.

Mr. Barrack towered over Jim. "What did he say to you?"

Jim forced himself to stand up, his legs trembling like reeds in the wind.

"He said he can't read, sir," he whispered, and had to shout it out a few times more until Mr. Barrack could hear him.

"Can't read!" the teacher bellowed. "Can't read! I'll say he can't read. What's the use of teaching boys like him to read? What do any of you want with reading or writing, miserable sinners that you are?" He pulled Tip's hand toward him again and lashed the rope across it.

Jim glanced at Tip, afraid to speak. He could see that the boy's eyes were wet and that he was nursing his hand under his armpit.

"Write!" Mr. Barrack barked, and Jim picked up his chalk and scribbled furiously with it, just as Tip had done.

At the end of that morning, Mr. Barrack told the boys to get out their instruments, and with a great shoving of desks and scuffle of boots they ran to the big cupboards at the end of the room, only to be shouted at and made to do it all again in silence.

"I'd have got hit anyway," Tip muttered to Jim under the noise. His eyes were still wet.

"Did it hurt?" Jim asked him.

Tip shook his head. "Once Barrack starts hitting you, Barrack always hits you," he said. He blew on his hand and stuck it back under his armpit. "Every day if he can. Just don't let him have a chance to start. Tell Barrack Tip did it, if he blames you for anything. Tip'll get hit anyway, so you might as well."

A drum was placed on the desk for them to share, and Tip stood up and reached out for a stick. At a wave of the schoolmaster's hand the hymn tune started, such a thumping and wailing that the washerwomen ran out with their hands over their ears. It was like nothing Jim had ever heard before.

Tip poked him with a drumstick and mouthed at him over the commotion to bang the other side of the drum with it. Jim just tapped it at first. He watched Tip to try to work out some kind of rhythm in the mess of noise, and he saw that all the boys seemed to be chanting something, the little black holes of their mouths opening and closing into the thunder of drums and whistles, while the candle flames flattened and danced like tiny white devils.

"What're you saying?" Jim shouted, as close to Tip's ear as he could get. Tip turned toward him.

"I hate this place!" Jim could hear Tip's voice, faint and wailing over the beating of his drum. He had his eyes shut. He thumped the drum in time to every word. "I *hate* this place!" Bang *bang* bang bang.

"So do I," said Jim. Bang bang bang. He closed his eyes and put his head back. He shouted into the darkness, opening up his throat to let all the tightness out. "I want Pa. I want Ma." Bang bang bang. "I want Emily." Bang bang bang. "I want Liz." Bang bang bang-bang *bang!* "I want to go *home!*"

Mr. Barrack raised his hand, and the sound stopped as if it had been torn away in shreds. Silence—utter, swirling, hugging silence. Jim felt his thoughts tumbling into it and then settling into calm. He felt better.

7

The Wild Thing

"Joseph," Jim asked the bent man one day out in the yard, "how long have you been here?"

"Been here?" Joseph swung his head around and peered up at Jim. "Seems like I was born here. Don't know nowhere else, son. And I don't know all of this place, neither." He leaned against Jim so that he could swing his head up to look at the long, high building with its rows of barred windows. "I've not been in the room where the women go, though long ago I must have been in the baby room, I suppose, with my ma. I've been in the infirmary wards. But there's all kinds of little twisty corridors and attics and places I've never been in, Jim, and I don't want to, neither. It's the whole world, this place is." He spread out his hands. "Whole world."

"It ain't, Joseph," Jim told him. "There's no shops here, and no carriages. And no trees." He closed his eyes, forcing himself to try to remember what it was like outside. "And there's no river. There's a great big river outside here."

"Is there, now?" said Joseph. "I should like to see that river. Though to tell you the truth, Jim, I don't know what a river is. Tell you something." He put his arm over Jim's shoulder to draw his ear closer to his own mouth. "I don't want to die in here. If someone will let me know what day I'm going to die, I'll be grateful. I'll climb over that wall first." He dropped his head down again and stared at his boots, whistling softly. "Yes. That's what I'll do."

Tip spluttered and nudged Jim, but Jim was looking up at the high walls that surrounded the workhouse, and at the bleak sky above it.

"How long have I been here, Tip?" he asked.

"How should I know?" Tip hugged his arms around himself. "Keep moving, Jim. It's cold."

It was impossible to tell one day from the next. They were all the same. School, sack making, bed. The only thing that changed was the sky. Jim had seen the gray of snow clouds turning into the soft rain clouds of spring. He'd felt summer scorching him in his heavy, itchy clothes. And now the sky was steely gray again. The pump had long beards of ice on its handle.

"I've been here a year," Jim said.

It was then that the little secret promise that had nestled inside him began to flutter into life like a wild thing.

I've got to skip off. He let the mad thought rise up in him. If I don't, I'll be like Joseph. One day I won't remember whether I was born here or not. I won't know anywhere but here.

During lessons that day the old schoolmaster's voice droned on in the dim schoolroom. The boys coughed and shuffled on their benches, hunching themselves against the cold.

Jim's wild thoughts drummed inside him, so loud that he imagined everyone would hear them. He leaned over to Tip and whispered in his ear, "Tip, I'm going to run away today. Come with me?"

Tip sheered around and put his hand to his mouth. Mr. Barrack sprang down from his chair, his eyes alight with anger and joy.

"You spoke!" he said to Jim, triumphant. "It was you."

Tip closed his eyes and held out his hand, but Jim stood up. He didn't mind. He didn't mind anything anymore. The teacher hauled him off his stool and swung his rope around. It hummed as it sliced through the air.

"I don't mind," Jim tried to explain, but this made Mr. Barrack angrier than ever. At last he had caught Jim out, and he was beating him now for every time he had tried and failed. He pulled a greasy handkerchief out of his pocket and wound it around Jim's head, tying it tight under his chin.

"Just in case you feels like hollering," he said. All the other boys stared in front of them. The rope stung Jim again and again, and the beating inside him was like a wild bird now, throbbing in his limbs and in his stomach, in his chest and in his head, so wild and loud that he felt it would lift him up and carry him away.

When the schoolmaster had finished with him, he

flung him like a bundle of rags across the desk. Jim lay in a shimmer of pain and thrumming wings. He wanted to sleep. The bell rang and the boys shuffled out. Jim felt Tip's hand on his shoulder. He flinched away.

"That's what they do to the boys who skip off, Jim," Tip whispered. "They thrash 'em like that every day until they're good."

Jim felt the wild thing fluttering again. "Only if they catch them."

"They always catch 'em. Bobbies catch 'em and bring 'em in, and they get thrashed and thrashed."

Jim struggled to sit up. The stinging rolled down his body. "Won't you come with me?"

"I daresn't. Honest, I daresn't. Don't go, Jim."

Jim looked up at the great archways of the schoolroom. He knew the words off by heart. *God is good. God is holy. God is just. God is love.*

"I've got to," he said. "And I'm going tonight, Tip."

8

The Carpet Beaters

Jim knew that he would have to make his break before old Marion did her rounds for the night. He had no idea how he was going to do it. At suppertime he stuffed his cheese into his pocket, and Tip passed his own share along to him.

At the end of the meal, Mr. Sissons stood up on his dais. All the shuffling and whispering stopped. He moved his body slowly around, which was his way of fixing his eyes on everyone, freezing them like statues.

"I'm looking for some big boys," he said, "to help the carpet beaters." He waited in the silence, but nobody moved.

"Just as I would expect. A rush to help, when there is sickness in the wards." A cold sigh seemed to ripple through the room. Mr. Sissons laughed into it in his dry, hissing way. "It might be cholera, my dears. That's what I hear. I've two thousand mouths to feed here, and someone has to earn the money, cholera or not. Somebody has to buy the medicines. Somebody has to pay for the burials." He moved his body around in its slow, watchful circle again. "Plenty of big strong boys here, eating every crumb I give them, and never a word of thanks." He stepped down from his dais and walked along the rows, cuffing some of the big boys on the backs of their heads as he passed them. "I want you all up in the women's wards straight after supper, and you don't come down again till all the carpets are done."

"What's carpets?" asked Jim.

"Dunno," Tip whispered. "They come from the rich houses, and the women here beat 'em, and then they send them home."

"I'm going with them," Jim said suddenly, standing up as soon as the older boys did.

"A daft boy, you are," said Tip. "He asked for big boys."

"You coming or not?" Jim darted off after the big boys, and Tip ran after him.

They were taken into one of the infirmary wards. As soon as he saw the people in their beds, Jim thought again about his mother. Was this the room she had been taken into the night they arrived? He wondered whether anyone would have remembered her coming, whether anyone had spoken to her.

The air was thick with dust and heavy with a rhythmic thudding sound. Lines had been strung from one end of the ward to the other, and carpets flung across them. Women and big boys with their sleeves rolled up were hitting the carpets with flattened sticks, and at every stroke the dust shivered in the air like clouds of flies. In their beds the sick people gasped and coughed and begged for water, and the old nurse shuffled from patient to patient and moaned with them and told them off in turns.

The woman in charge of the carpet beaters came down the row and stood with her hands on her hips, watching Tip and Jim. The boys stood on their toes, trying to reach the middles of the carpets with their sticks. Jim was still so stiff from his beating that he could hardly flex his shoulders.

"Now who sent you two along!" The woman laughed. "Might as well get a pair of spiders to come and do the job!"

Jim staggered back, exhausted, and let the beating-stick drop. "We're really strong, though," he said. "Look!" and he bent his arm back, squeezing his fist to try to make a muscle bulge. "And we'd do anything to help Mr. Sissons, wouldn't we, Tip?"

"You're supposed to thrash the carpets, not tickle them." The woman bent down suddenly and scooped Jim up in her arms. "Oh, you're a big boy, you are!" She pressed him to her. "Not too big for a cuddle?"

Jim struggled to get himself free again, and the woman laughed and lowered him down.

"Need a ma, you do," she said, smoothing her apron. "Like I need a little boy. Lost mine. Soon as I came in here, lost my little boy. But who'd want to bring up a child in here, eh?"

"Come on, Jim," said Tip, embarrassed. "We could go back to the sewing room and do our sacks."

"But we want to help," Jim said. "We're good at carrying, ain't we, Tip?"

"Are you, now?" the woman said. "Well then, before you go, you can just help me carry this carpet out to the yard. The man's out there waiting with his cart."

She hoisted up a long, rolled-up carpet by the middle and nodded to Jim and Tip to take each end. Between them they managed to get it past the beds and the beaters and down a winding staircase. At the end of the corridor the matron sat by the doorway, knitting a black shawl. Without looking at them, she unlocked the door and sank back into the dim pool of her candlelight to carry on with her knitting.

And outside the door were the railings and the gate.

Jim knew it was the gate he had come in by, all those months ago. He could smell air, miles and miles of air. He could hear the voices of ordinary people in the street outside. He could hear the cries of the city.

A man stood just inside the gate with a cart, and when the carpet woman called out to him, he came toward them to help, calling something out to her that made her laugh.

"Now, you can run back in, boys," the woman said, pushing her hair under her cap. "And straight back to your sack making, mind. No more carpet beating for you, little spiders, till you're twice your size. Don't you think so, Thomas?"

Her voice was light and laughing, but the boys could see by the way she turned her smiling face up toward the man that he was a friend of hers and that she was far more interested in him than she was in them. When she followed him to the shadows under the wall, they knew that she had forgotten all about them.

And Jim's wild thing was thudding in his chest.

"Tip . . . ," he whispered. There was the gate, wide open, with the cart halfway inside it. There was the road, and the gleam of lamplights, and the clopping of horses' hooves. He felt a rearing of fear and excitement inside him. This was the moment. He felt for his friend's hand and gripped it tight.

"I daresn't. I daresn't," Tip whispered back. "Don't forget me, Jim."

His hand slipped off. Far away in the back of his mind, Jim heard the scuff of boots on the snow and knew that Tip had run back into the house.

Jim crept forward, invisible in the deep shadows, and stood, hardly breathing, just inside the gate. He heard the carpet woman laughing quietly, and at that moment he took his chance. He slinked himself like a cat into a thin, small shape, and glided out through the gate. He tiptoed along the other side of the railings and stood with his breath in his mouth till a cart rumbled past. He darted out behind it and ran alongside it until he was well past the workhouse, till his breath was bursting out of him. At last he fell, weak and panting, into the black well of a side alley.

He was free.

9

The Jaw of the
Iron Dog

Jim knew one thing for sure: He must keep away from policemen. If they see me, they'll send me back, he thought. He remembered the white-faced boys in the yard. But I'll run away again as soon as I get a chance.

Somewhere in his head was the thought of finding Rosie again. She had been his mother's friend. Maybe, if he found her, he would find Emily and Lizzie, too. But London was a huge, throbbing, noisy place. He had no idea which way to go. The shops were still open and busy, and the streets were full of traders carrying trays of fish and fruit, shouting out their wares. A woman was selling coffee from a handcart. The smell of it reminded him of that morning in the kitchen of the big house, when Rosie had given his mother some of his lordship's coffee to drink.

The night noises of the street baffled Jim—he had grown used to the drowning quiet of the workhouse, and the distant midnight wails of the mad people. Out here, it seemed as if no one wanted to sleep.

He reckoned he was probably safer where there were many people around. Lots of boys of about his age were dodging about from one side of the street to the other, in and out of the light of the lamps. It was easy to pretend to be one of them. Soon he stopped to rest against a shop wall, leaning next to another boy. He slid his hand into his pocket for a bit of his supper cheese. The boy looked at him, and Jim stuffed the cheese into his mouth before he had a chance to grab it.

"You from the workhouse?" the boy asked him.

Jim shook his head.

"Bet you are. Them's workhouse clothes, ain't they?"

The boy was dressed in tattered trousers and a torn, thin jacket, but the cap on his head was the same as Jim's. Before Jim could speak to him, the boy snatched up a broom that was propped beside him and darted out to stand beside a man in a top hat and long coat.

"Clear the road for you, sir?" he said, and when the man nodded, the boy stepped out in front of him, brushing a pathway through the slush. The man tossed him a coin without looking at him. Jim ran after the boy.

"Give us your clothes, and you can have mine," he offered.

The boy laughed at him. "Not likely!" He darted off with his broom across his shoulders.

There was a sudden cackle of voices behind Jim. A woman selling pickled salmon was being shouted at by another woman with a tray of eels around her waist. Onlookers were joining in, and bearing down on them, their tall hats visible over all the heads, were two policemen. Jim put his head down and ran.

Soon he realized that he was out of the busy area, and that he was running through quiet streets without shops. The roads were wider here, and the houses grand. They began to look familiar, and yet it was impossible to tell one from another. He came to a dark square that was full of skinny trees. In the middle of it was a fountain, and, as if he had looked through a window into his memory, he knew that he had been here before.

He sat down on the fountain steps. He had sat here on that last journey when his mother had stopped to drink. He had trailed his hands in the water. A bit farther on, he thought, there should be a statue of a man on a horse. He made himself stand up, hardly daring to look. There it was. The very statue. They had stopped there, too. She had leaned against the statue, and he had seen the fountain and helped her across to it. She had been so weak then that she could have been a little child. He remembered how helpless and frightened he had felt. And that had been over a year ago.

He could hardly believe that it was a whole year since his mother had died. Emily and Lizzie didn't even know. All these things were just as they had been then—the man on the horse and the fountain and the big houses. Only this time, his mother wasn't here.

He walked slowly up to the statue. Three streets led away from it—three long, tree-lined streets—and one of them was the street where Rosie worked. If he found Rosie, he would find Emily and Lizzie again. He began to run.

The houses all looked the same. They all had black railings and a little flight of steps going up to the main door, and a little flight leading down to the servants' quarters. Must he knock on every door in every street until he found the right one? He ran up the first street, then came back and tried the second. A sound caught his attention, and he looked around. Hanging from the window of one of the kitchens was a tiny cage. A finch with just enough room to move hopped from stand to floor to stand again, whistling out loud for a companion. Jim had heard that before. He was in the right street, and somewhere, a long way up it, was the house he was searching for.

By the time he stopped again, he knew exactly what to look out for. He remembered, when his mother had sunk down on the steps, and Lizzie had looked up at the grand house and asked if that was where they were going to live, he had seen something that had made him hope it wasn't. On the side of the step there had been a metal boot scraper in the shape of a dog's head, with a wide, vicious mouth. He remembered thinking then that if he had put his foot inside the mouth, the metal teeth would have come clashing together and pinned him there for good. He ran from side to side of the street looking for it, and at last, there it was. He had found it.

The house upstairs was in darkness, but down in the basement window was the soft glow of a candle. He tumbled down the steps, tripping himself up in his big boots, and fell against the door.

"Emily! Emily!" he shouted out. Before he could raise his fist to hammer on the door, it was pulled open, and he staggered against a girl.

10

Lame Betsy

"We don't give to beggars," the girl said, trying to edge him out of the door again with her knee.

"I'm looking for Emily."

"Emily? There's no Emily here."

"Emily Jarvis. She helps Rosie out in the kitchen."

"Rosie? Who's she?" The girl was laughing down at him through her loose hair.

"Rosie," Jim said. "You must know Rosie. She's got big arms. And she don't like making bread."

The girl burst out laughing and looked over her shoulder at a woman who was sewing by the table.

"Hear that?" she said. "There's no one here who doesn't like making bread, is there?" She laughed again, and the other woman laughed back in a mocking sort of way.

Jim peered past the girl. Surely it was the right kitchen. It had to be.

"You'll have to go, sonny," the girl said. "You've snooped around for long enough, I reckon."

"There was a lady with a black crinkly dress," Jim said. "Called Judd. She'll remember."

"Judd!" the other woman said. She put her sewing down. "She was the last housekeeper. She was sent away. And there was another woman, too—the cook. I got her job. They were found hiding some street children in the kitchen, and his lordship dismissed them."

"They were my sisters," said Jim. The drumming in his head was so loud that he could hardly hear his own voice. "Emily and Lizzie. Please, miss, where are they? Where's Rosie?"

The cook stood up and came to the doorway. She stood with her arms folded, frowning out at Jim. Her face softened when she saw him in the light.

"Are they workhouse clothes?" she asked.

"Please don't send me back there," Jim begged.

"I wouldn't send my worst enemy there," the cook said. "You go off to bed," she said to the girl. "I'll put him on his way."

The girl, who seemed to think it was all a fine joke, tweaked Jim's cap over his eye and took her candle up the side stairs that led to the servants' quarters. The cook drew Jim in and told him to sit by the fire.

"Lucky for you," she said, "his lordship's away for the night. If he was here, you wouldn't set foot over this doorstep, or we'd all be off to the workhouse. And lucky for you I've decided to stay up and get this sewing done. And don't think you can steal anything."

Jim shook his head, afraid to speak.

"Don't you dare move from that spot." She put her glasses on the end of her nose and glared at Jim as he squirmed in the chair. The heat from the kitchen made him drowsy. He slid his hand into his pocket and felt for the last of his cheese. It had gone, and he knew that the boy sweeping the road had taken it. He tipped the last few bread crumbs into the palm of one hand.

Without saying anything, the woman put down her sewing and ladled some stew from the big pot on the hearth. She pushed the bowlful in front of him and winked without smiling, and Jim did his best to wink back. He ate in silence, and she sewed in silence, frowning at her needle as she rethreaded it, glancing at Jim over the tops of her glasses from time to time.

Gradually he sank asleep. Sometimes during the night, he woke up and heard a little soft purring sound, and knew that the cook was snoring into her pile of sewing, but then she would wake up with a snort, and Jim would drift away again. And at last they were both startled out of their sleep by a sharp rapping on the glass and a voice calling out, "Half-past five, time to be alive!" and there was the knocker-upper hobbling past the window on his morning rounds, and Jim and the cook were awake for good.

She sent him out to the backyard to fetch in water and sticks, and got the fire going and a pot of water boiling on the hearth. The girl came downstairs, yawning like a cat, and scratched Jim's head as she passed him.

"You still here?"

"He's going any minute," the cook said. "Soon as the dairywoman comes, he's on her cart and away, and he's never coming back. That right?"

Jim nodded. He wished they would ask him to stay. He liked the warm kitchen and the winking cook, and most of all he liked her warm, sweet-smelling bread. If only Emily and Lizzie were here, too, this would be a fine place to stay.

They heard a bell ringing out in the street, and the cook picked up a couple of jugs. "Here's Lame Betsy now."

Jim followed her out to the road and up the steps. Lame Betsy was leading a knock-kneed horse from house to house, selling milk from a slopping churn on the cart.

"This boy," said the cook, pushing Jim forward, "is looking for Rosie, and if I'm right, she's a friend of yours, Betsy."

The dairywoman grunted and pushed her hair under her cap. She ladled milk into the cook's jugs, her breath coming thick and slow.

"She's gone down in the world, Rosie Trilling has," she said. "Nice job she had here, and now she's selling whelks for her grandfather. All because of a couple of street kids."

"This boy's sisters, they were," the cook put in, and Betsy set down the jugs and pushed her hair into her cap again.

"Were they now? Doesn't seem right, does it?" she

went on. "Just for helping people out like that. Your sisters, were they? Didn't look like street kids to me." Her hair floated free again as she shook her head, thick gray strands of it dipping into the milk as she ladled it out of its churn. "She was a fine woman, your ma, or so Rosie said."

Jim couldn't look at her. He reached up to pat the horse's bony head, and it snorted and pulled back its lips, scaring him. "What happened to Emily and Lizzie?" He couldn't bring himself to look at Lame Betsy. He was frightened of what her answer might be.

She shifted her weight from one leg to the other. "Don't ask me that, because I don't know," she said. "If you wants to climb on the cart, I'll take you to your Rosie. But where the girls is, I don't know, and that's the truth."

Jim scrambled up onto the cart, slippery and sour-smelling with milk. The cook said something to the kitchen girl lounging against the railings, and she ran down the steps into the kitchen. She came back up again with a small loaf in her hands. She passed it to Jim, laughing up at his surprise. It was still warm. He tried to thank the cook with a wink, but she turned away.

"Don't you dare come back," she said. "There's nothing we can do for you." Her voice had gone thick in her throat. "God bless you, child. I hope he takes care of you." And she hurried away without looking back at him.

Jim spent the morning jolting from side to side on the cart, jumping down from time to time to help Betsy heave the horse over sticky heaps of snow.

"There's my yard," Betsy grunted to him at one point. "And there's my cows. Hear them talking to each other? Like old men in an alehouse they are, full of wind and wisdom. Now, this is where my round finishes, but if Albert will let you, we'll carry on to the river."

Jim jumped down again, and they both hauled on Albert's reins until they'd coaxed him past Betsy's yard and the mumbling of the cows.

"Let's smell your bread, Jim," Betsy said. He had already nibbled the end of it and was keen to save the rest for his next few meals. Betsy reached out for it and took a huge bite, her loose teeth bending forward as she chewed it.

"Poor old Rosie Trilling," she kept sighing in her breathy voice. "Poor old Rosie."

They were coming near the river. Jim could smell it, and he could hear the gulls keening across it. The street they were in now was littered with the heads and spines of fish, and women sat on crates gossiping as they worked at their filleting. Their hands were slimy and red with fish entrails. Cats and children prowled around them.

A dairywoman with her pails slung across her shoulders on a yoke trudged past them and shouted out something at Betsy. Betsy clicked at Albert to stop.

"She'll be gutting me," she grunted, "if she thinks I'm

selling milk on her patch. Hop down, Jimmy, and ask someone where Rosie Trilling lives. Someone'll know her."

Jim slid down from the cart and watched Lame Betsy coaxing her horse around and limping back along the street.

I could stay with her, he thought, if I don't find Rosie. I could milk her cows for her and carry her pails. Surely she could give me a home.

He started after her. "Betsy . . . ," he called, but she didn't hear him. She and the younger dairywoman were shouting at each other across the street, while the knock-kneed horse nosed into the muddy road and snorted at the fish heads.

Jim ran down the side street. The houses backed onto the river and had boats in their yards, spars and masts rocking gently, tinkling in the early breeze. Men were edging barges out, shouting across to one another, their voices bouncing off the buildings and echoing over the water. Some women were standing, hands on hips, watching them.

Jim couldn't remember what Rosie looked like anymore. In his mind he saw a big woman with floury hands and her hair neat under a white cap, a starched apron tied over her long black dress. There was no one here like that. The women he saw had drab shawls draped across their heads and shoulders, and wore coarse dresses with ragged hems. He listened to their voices, trying to pick out one that he recognized, but they all sounded the same, pitched to shriek against the bustling noises of barges on the move and the screaming of gulls.

At last he plucked up the courage to ask someone where Rosie Trilling lived.

"If she's in," he was told, "she's at the white cottage at the bottom end."

When he knocked at the door, a woman's voice shouted to him to come in, and he knew it was Rosie's.

And she was there, crouching over a brazier that was glowing with hot coals, coaxing flames out of it. She was holding a twisted wire with a glistening herring skewered to it. An old woman, wrapped in bundles of brown and gray shawls, huddled next to her in a chair that seemed to be made out of boxes roped together. Rosie was breaking bits off the herring and feeding the old woman with it. She looked up at Jim, surprised.

"The men have set off, son," she told him.

"Rosie," said Jim. His eyes stung from the smoke. He rubbed them with the backs of his hands.

"Yes, I'm Rosie," she said. "And I told you—"

"I've come about Lizzie and Emily," he said. The smoke seemed to be in his throat now, twisting down inside him. It was hard for him to breathe. "I'm Jim Jarvis."

"Lord bless us." Rosie dropped the herring into the flames, where it spurted like a blue light. The old woman swore at her.

"Annie's little boy?" Rosie stared at him, her hand to her mouth.

Jim nodded. He bit the back of his hand to try to make the stinging in his eyes go away. He could hardly see Rosie. Now she was a brown, blurred shape that was moving around the brazier and coming toward him. She smelled of warmth and fish. She squatted down to his level, putting her hands on his shoulders.

"Ma died. A long time ago," Jim began.

Rosie pressed him to her and ran her hands through his hair, hugging him as if he were a tiny child again, and for the very first time since Joseph had told him the terrible news, Jim let out all the hurt he'd held locked up inside him and cried for his mother.

11

The Spitting Crow

Rosie sat on the floor and rocked Jim until he had sobbed himself to sleep, and then she lowered him down and went outside. The old woman stuck out her foot and tried to nudge Jim awake, but he was just too far away for her to reach. She spat into the fire instead.

Rosie had gone down the yard to a shed that was built out over the river. Foul-smelling water lapped under it. Inside, it was heaped with bits of yarn and tarred ropes, but she managed to push those to one end to make a bed, of a sort, out of old sacks. She went back into the cottage and filled a tray with whelks and eels that she was going to sell down near the shops, and hurried out. She knew that if Jim woke up he wouldn't wander far, and she also knew that she couldn't afford to miss the morning shoppers.

The old grandmother edged her box chair closer and at last managed to kick Jim awake. He sat up slowly, puzzled to find himself in this strange, smoky room with a toothless old woman peering down at him. Then he remembered where he was. He was in Rosie's cottage, and he was safe.

The old woman nudged him again with her boot and nodded toward the half-eaten loaf that was sticking out of his pocket. She stretched out her clawed hand, and Jim broke off a piece of bread and held it out to her, afraid of her glaring eyes and her restless, chewing mouth. She scowled at him and pecked at his hand, then opened her mouth wide. Jim broke off another bit of bread and fed it to her, and like a greedy bird she pecked and waited, and he fed her bit by bit. Sometimes, when she was slow, he bit a piece off for himself.

When she nodded off to sleep, he wandered outside and sat by the river. It was as busy as a market, with sailing ships plowing their way through the mist, and barges nudging in and out of the wharves. Far out he could just make out the bulk of a paddle steamer, huge and wheezing. He wondered how far the river went, and what it would be like to be on one of those boats, rocking in the wake of the steamers.

When Rosie came home, it was nearly dark again. Jim stayed outside all the time, a little afraid of the spitting grandmother and her greedy, pecking mouth. Quite a few people seemed to go into the cottage, mostly men and boys. From time to time Jim could hear the sound of arguing and shouting. One old man seemed to come and go a lot, and did most of the shouting, whether there was anyone else with him or not. When he wasn't shouting, he was laughing to himself, in a dry, coughing way that wasn't laughing at all. Jim wondered if he was Rosie's grandfather.

It was cold out on the bankside, but Jim didn't want to go back into the cottage. He watched some boys playing in the snow and tried to join in, but they ran away as soon as they saw him. When at last he saw Rosie coming, he ran to her. The tray that she had strapped to her shoulders was half-empty. She dragged her feet as she walked.

"Well, Jim," she said, "I've no time to talk to you now. I've food to cook for my grandfather and my uncles, as they're kind enough to give me a home." She stopped by the cottage. "And I can't ask you in. Grandfather would throw you to the gulls, and me with you, if he thought you were intending to stay. There's too many of us. Do you understand?"

Jim stared up at her.

"Don't look at me like that, Jim," she said. "You don't know my grandfather, or you wouldn't look at me like that. But I'll show you where you can sleep tonight, if you promise to be careful."

She took him down to the shed. "Will you be all right here?" she asked. "It's cold, and it don't half stink with all that rot on the river, but it's dry enough."

"I like it," said Jim. "I can pretend I'm on a boat, Rosie."

"So you can." She stood at the door and looked out at the darkening water as if she'd never seen it before, her eyes narrowing. "Like to sail away, would you, Jim? I know I would. Far away to anywhere. Anywhere would be better than this. Drowning would be better than this." She turned around abruptly. "You bed down then, and I'll bring you some cooked fish in a bit."

Jim could hear shouting from the cottage when Rosie went down to it. He could hear the old pecky woman crowing for food and the grandfather coughing. Nobody seemed to talk quietly. From all the cottage doors and windows along the wharves there spilled out the sounds of shouting and arguing. Jim remembered the quiet of the wards and wondered whether Tip was asleep by now, and whether he was missing him.

Later Rosie brought hot fish and tea and bread, and a candle in a holder for him. Jim had been lying on his stomach watching the boat lanterns glimmering like eyes on the water, as if they were creatures turning themselves upside down in the darkness. She knelt down and tucked the sacking around him.

"Don't you ever let Grandpa know you're here. See?"

"I won't."

"Good boy. I'll go in soon, and see to the old lady."

"She's like a sparrow," said Jim.

Rosie laughed. "A crow, more like. Seen crows, Jim? Flappy, greedy things? That's Grandma, when she gets going. A spitting crow. I sometimes think she'd peck my hand right off if she was hungry enough."

"Rosie," said Jim. "Can I stay here?"

She held the candle up so that she could look down at him. "Stay here? I don't know how long I'll be staying here myself."

"Can't you ever go back to his lordship's house?"

"I wish I could! I was very comfortable there. I was very lucky to get that job. It was because Lame Betsy spoke up for me that I got it. But never mind. I lost it, and that's that."

"Was it because of Lizzie and Emily that you lost it?"

Rosie was silent for a bit. Then she said, "Lord, no. Whatever made you think that, Jim? It was because my cooking was so bad! I've never cooked anything but fish in my life! And they expected me to bake bread. Bread! My bread broke the flagstones if I dropped it."

Jim smiled to himself in the darkness. He'd just tried some of Rosie's bread and he reckoned she was right.

"But what about Emily and Lizzie? They didn't get sent to the workhouse, did they?"

Rosie blew her nose on her fishy apron. "To the workhouse? Emily and Lizzie? I'd have fought them all, his lordship included, if they'd done that. No, I'll tell you what happened to Emily and Lizzie. Close your eyes, and I'll tell you what happened."

Jim listened quietly while Rosie told him about a gray-eyed lady who had visited the big house. She had come right down into the kitchen to see the two girls for herself. "She took them upstairs, Jim, and had them washed in her own washroom. And she sent out for dresses for them—a blue one for Emily, and a white one for Lizzie. And then she took them in a carriage, a beautiful carriage drawn by four white horses. You should have seen them setting off, as proud as little queens! They went all the way to the countryside, to her summer home, to be looked after there."

She tucked the sacks around him and crept out of the shed and back to the noisy cottage, and Jim lay for a long time listening to the soft lapping of the river against his shed, thinking about the story Rosie had told him. And hoping it was true.

12

Shrimps

Next morning Rosie told Jim that he would have to help her if she was going to feed him. She tied an old sack over his shoulders to disguise the workhouse clothes, in case the police saw him.

"You'll have to keep moving, Jim, same as me," she warned him. "If the bobbies see me standing still, they'll soon pack me off as well. We'll both be running all day."

Jim liked working for her. When her voice grew tired, he would shout out for her, "Whelkso! Salmon for sale! Pickled fish and shrimpso!" He danced around while he was shouting, partly to keep himself warm and partly so that he could watch out on all sides for policemen coming. He had such a light, skipping way of dancing that people stopped to watch him on their way to their shops and offices. They soon got to know him.

"Skip for us, Jimmy!" they used to say, especially if they saw him standing on his own.

"Buy some shrimps and I will!" Jim would say, and Rosie would step up with her tray of seafood and persuade them to buy something. While they were eating, Jim would dance for them, and he would close his eyes, close out the street, and close out the faces of all the strangers. . . .

A long time ago his father had danced for him in their cottage. Jim could just remember the laughing faces of Emily and Lizzie as they sat on a long polished bench by the fire. He had been a very small boy then. He remembered clapping his hands and shouting out as his father danced, and the faster his father jumped, the more the flames in the fire had danced, like wild, yellow spirits. "Faster, Pa! Faster!" the children had shouted, and the black shadow that leaped from his father's feet had become a crazy, long-limbed, prancing shape across the walls and the ceiling, and Jim had jumped down and run to do a skipping dance with him, and been lifted up to the beams. There he was, in the room again, while strangers watched him and ate Rosie's seafood in the cold street.

"I'm very pleased with you, Skipping Jim," Rosie told him, breaking into his dream. "I'm selling more salmon than I can pickle. They'll have to have it boiled plain if they want more, and like it!"

He had been staying with Rosie a few days when he first saw the doctor. He and Rosie were going back to her cottage one afternoon when they heard a voice behind them calling, "Rosie! Rosie Trilling!" and they turned around to see Lame Betsy limping after them, holding up her skirts as she tried to hurry through the mud.

"I've been worriting about that boy," Betsy panted. "Whether he'd find you, and whether you could give him a home, and how he was doing."

"He's doing fine." Rosie laughed. "He's a real little dancing man, ain't you, Jim? But he can't stay with me for long, he knows that. I'm in mortal fear of my grandfather finding him and throwing us both out. You know what he's like, Betsy."

Betsy stuffed her loose hair back under her cap. "Well, I've got a fine plan!" She held out her hand, plump and pink with cold. "You come with me, Jim. I'm going to take you to school!"

Jim's stomach churned with terror. "I hate school!" he shouted. "I hate schoolteachers!" He tried to pull himself away from Betsy.

"He's not a schoolteacher, Jim. He's a doctor, so they say. And he's a school going for the likes of you, Jim. He's a queer soul, they say, and he stands on a box in the middle of the street and asks people to bring their children along to his school, and he don't charge them nothing!" She stopped for breath, banging her chest with her fist. She held out her hand again. "Come on, Jim! It's a fine chance for you!"

Jim felt tears scorching. "Please don't make me! Don't make me go to school!"

But Rosie pushed him gently toward Betsy. "Go with her, Jim," she said. "Somewhere to go where you'll be warm and dry. And it's free! Wish I had a chance to go to school!"

"But I want to help you, Rosie!" Jim called out, but Rosie hurried away from them.

Betsy pulled him along with her, squeezing out comforting words between her breathy wheezings.

"You'll hear Bible stories, I should think, and sing lots of nice hymns. I don't want you getting into bad ways, Jim, just because you ain't got a mother and father. Look at that crowd! That'll be him, talking now."

Betsy pushed Jim to the front of the staring crowd. A thin man with spectacles and fluffy side-whiskers was standing on a box, turning from side to side. He spoke in a light, soft voice with an Irish accent, which Jim could hardly understand. Some of the people watching him were laughing, and a group of ragged boys were jeering. The man didn't seem to hear them, but just kept on talking in his gentle voice. Jim strained to hear what he was saying, and then caught the words that he dreaded. It was almost as if he had been hauled by the scruff of his neck into the long, dim schoolroom in the workhouse, with Mr. Barrack slicing the air with his whistling rope.

"God is love," said the doctor. "God is good."

"No, he ain't!" Jim shouted. "He ain't good to me!"

Everybody broke into a roar of cheering laughter and shouts. One of the boys on the corner picked up a lump of mud and flung it at the doctor. It landed with a splash across his face, stopping up his mouth as he opened it to speak again. The doctor coughed and wiped his mouth on his sleeve. He was jostled off his crate. He pushed his way through the crowd, struggling to keep his hat on his head. As he passed Jim, he looked at him, just for a second, and what Jim saw in his eyes wasn't anger, or reproach, but sadness.

Jim turned away. Betsy was wiping her eyes on her sleeve. "Go on!" She laughed. "Back to your Rosie, you vagabond! There's not much you don't know!"

Jim raced off through the alleyways to find Rosie. He was followed by some of the boys from the crowd. "Hey, Skipping Jim!" they shouted. "Wait for us!"

But Jim didn't stop until he had found Rosie again. The boys panted up to him, cuffing him lightly with their fists to show they wanted to be friends.

"Come on, Skipping Jim. Dance for us!" they shouted, and they stood about in their tattered clothes, hugging themselves against the cold, while Jim capered around to make them laugh.

"You'll soon wear those boots out," Rosie warned him. "Save your dancing for the proper customers."

But Jim wanted to dance for the boys. They didn't often laugh. There wasn't much for them to laugh at. He was always too shy to talk to them. But after that day when he had made them laugh at the doctor, they often came to watch him dance in the streets.

One of them was a red-haired, poky sort of boy. He reminded Jim of Tip, just a bit. His hair was bright and untidy, and it poked out of the holes of the cap he wore on the side of his head. His toes wriggled like cold pink shrimps out of the ends of his boots, and his shirt hung off his skinny arms like tattered sails hanging off the spars of a ship. He made a sort of living selling bootlaces.

"Bootlaces, mister!" he shouted at passersby, whirling the laces above his head as if he were a ribbon seller at a fair. "Three for the price of two! You don't want three, sir? Well, two for the price of three then—can't say fairer than that, can I?"

When Jim was skipping, the boy would sit with his mouth wide open, as if he were afraid to laugh out loud. His eyes darted around, furtive, on the lookout all the time for likely customers, or for the police, or for something to help himself to. He would suddenly leap up and dash past a stall when the owner wasn't looking, and grab a lump of cheese or the broken end of a pie or a hot muffin. He'd run into a dark corner and stuff his cheeks full with it. Jim reckoned he must swallow it whole, it would disappear so fast.

If the stallholders saw him doing it, they usually swore loudly at him or chased him, but sometimes they saw him coming and looked the other way. It never occurred to Jim, watching him, that one day he would be doing this, too, and be thankful to steal enough crumbs in a day to keep himself alive.

Jim liked the look of this boy. A few times he went over to him to say something, but the boy would just run off as soon as Jim came near, as if he'd just remembered a job that needed doing. Jim would feel awkward then, and would pretend to be searching for something on the ground where the boy had been squatting. But every day he thought, I'll talk to him today. I'll find out what he's called, that's what.

One evening, just as dark was coming, the lad was sitting, watching Jim in his nervous, foxlike way, when a raggedy woman crept up behind him. She put her hands on his shoulders and shook him.

"Gotcha!" she said. "You bin hiding, aincha?"

He jumped up, trying to get away, but she pushed him to the ground and pinned him there with her knee on his chest. Her hair was as wild and red as his, and her voice thick and slurred.

"Where's yer money?" she demanded.

"Ain't got none," the boy said.

She flipped him over as if he were a wooden doll, felt in his back pockets, and held up some coins. "Now you've got none." She laughed, and before he could sit up, she'd gone.

Jim had been crouching on the other side of the road, watching. The boy saw him looking and turned away, covering up his face with his hands. He stayed hunched up just as the woman had left him. Jim stood up and clicked his fingers to make the boy look at him. Then he started to dance, just a few skipping steps. Laugh, he wanted to say, but didn't dare. It's all right. Laugh.

It was then that the boy seemed to make up his mind about him. He jumped up and joined Jim, kicking up his legs in imitation of Jim's dance, holding his arms high above his head so that his laces fluttered around like maypole ribbons. His pink shrimpy toes wriggled above the flaps of his boot soles, and with each step he took, he slapped his foot down again so firmly on the road that the muck spattered around him like flies around a cow. He danced with his eyes closed and his mouth wide open, in a kind of trance, and the more the watchers clapped, the wilder his dance became. Jim could hardly keep up with him for laughing, and even Rosie had to smile. She sold off most of her trayload to one family.

"Here," she said. "Shrimps, or whatever your name is. And you, Skipping Jim. You can finish off these for me—I'm going back to get some more. I've never sold two whole trayfuls like that in one day, never. You should go on the shows, you two! You should join a traveling circus!"

The two boys sat side by side near a night watchman's fire, peeling the shrimps with their teeth and spitting off the shells.

"I love shrimps, I do," said the boy. "But I've never pinched none off Rosie's stall, never."

"You wouldn't dare," said Jim. "She'd pickle you if you did."

"I dare do anyfink, I do," the boy said. "But Rosie, she's like me. She ain't got no more money than me, she ain't."

"Are you really called Shrimps?" Jim asked him.

The boy shrugged. "Shrimps is what they call me, and Shrimps'll do."

"Sounds like a funny name to me," Jim said. "Who was that woman?"

The boy narrowed his eyes. "My ma," he said. "Only she kicked me out years ago, didn't she? She only comes looking for me when she wants money for gin. Not much of a ma, she ain't."

"Where d'you live, then?"

"Depends, don't it? See, if I makes a copper or two selling laces, I spends it on a lodging house for the night."

"Cor. On your own?"

"On me own and wiv about fifty other geysers wot snore their heads off all night! It's like a funderstorm sometimes! And if I don't have no money"—he shrugged—"I sleeps where I can, don't I? Where the bobbies won't find me, that's where I live." He jerked his thumb at Jim's jacket, where the sacking shawl had slipped away. "I spent a week in that place. Worse'n anyfink I ever knowed, that workhouse was. Worse'n sleeping in a barn full of rats, and I done that a time or two."

"Worse than that," Jim agreed. "Worse than sleeping in a sack full of eels."

The boys both giggled.

"Eels!" snorted Shrimps. "Eels is charming company. I ate an eel once, when it were still alive. It wriggled all down my throat and round my belly and up again and out through my mouth! 'Bellies!' said the eel. 'Boys' bellies is nearly as bad as the workhouse!' And it wriggled off home. It was all right, that eel." He wiped his mouth with the back of his hand and looked at Jim sideways. "You got a bruvver, Skippin' Jim?"

"No," said Jim. "Have you?"

"Used to have. But I ain't got one now." Shrimps dug the flaps of his boot soles into the mud. "I'd like a bruvver to go round wiv."

"So would I," said Jim.

The two boys stared straight ahead, saying nothing.

The watchman poked his fire so that the flames hissed. He got slowly to his feet. "Five of the clock," he shouted, and trudged off to light up the lamps between the houses. "Five o'clock, my lovelies!"

"Got to go," Shrimps said. "I got a queue to see to. People often breaks their bootlaces when they're standing in queues. Just snaps off, they do, if I crawls round and tweaks 'em when they ain't looking."

"Will you be here tomorrow?"

Shrimps looked down at Jim. He took a bunch of laces out of his pocket and swirled them around his head. Then he shrugged and ran off.

That night, as Jim ran home to his shed, his head was busy with new thoughts. There was easily enough room for another small boy to squeeze in. It would be warmer with two of them. Rosie wouldn't mind, especially if Shrimps got his food in his usual way. Be nice to have a brother, he thought as he ran. A brother like Shrimps. Real nice, that would be.

Jim's sleep was broken by a stomping of boots and the screech the catch gave as the door was pulled open.

The sudden shock of cold was as if someone had let the river in.

A candle was held out toward him, and Jim opened his eyes. Two men stood looking down at him, their eyes black holes in the candlelight, their beards froths of fur. Jim recognized one as Rosie's grandfather. The other man was square, with a boxlike face and hair that slanted across his eyes like a slipping thatch.

"This boy, d'you mean?" He gave Jim a kick. Jim sat up in fright, clutching his sack around him.

"I knew I'd seen a lad running in here," Rosie's grandfather wheezed. "A little rat, he is, skulking in my shed. I'll weasel him out, I thought to myself. I'll winkle him out when the time is right."

"Please, mister," said Jim. "I ain't doin' no harm."

"Stand up," the square man said. His eyes bulged above his fat cheeks as if they were lamps trying to make their way through the thatch.

Jim struggled to his feet.

"He's only a twig," the square man said. "There's no bones in him, hardly."

"He'll grow," said the grandfather. "I know his type. He'll grow big and powerful. You can train him up, Nick, when he's only that big. Won't give you no trouble, that size. He's just right. And while he's training, he won't eat much."

Nick grunted. "Well, he's here, and I'm stuck for a boy, so I'll take him."

Grandfather sighed with pleasure. Nick fumbled in

his pocket and gave him a coin, which the old man held out to the candle, chuckling.

"Come on, boy," Nick said. "Bring your bed. You'll need that."

Jim stumbled after him, pulling the sack around his shoulders for warmth, and the door screeched behind him as the old man fastened it shut.

"Tell Rosie—," Jim began, but Grandpa swung around and snarled at him.

"She won't need no telling. I'll thank her, shall I, for stealing food from her grandmother's mouth to stuff in yours? Go on. Go with Grimy Nick. You've got a home and a job now. You've nothing more to want in life, that's what."

He walked slowly back to his cottage, laughing aloud in his coughing way, spinning the coin that Grimy Nick had given him so that it gleamed in the air like a little sun.

13

The *Lily*

Jim didn't dare ask where he was going, or whether he would be coming back, or if he could just run back to the cottage to say good-bye to Rosie. He was quite sure that Grandpa would tell her nothing. He imagined her hurrying out to him in the morning with a mug of tea and a chunk of her solid bread, trying the locked door, calling out to him. He imagined Shrimps swinging his bootlaces over his head, dancing in the streets without him, waiting. He hung back, wanting to dodge into the shadows and run off, but as if he could read his thoughts, Grimy Nick swung out his arm and grabbed him by the collar. Jim hurried beside Nick, stealing quick glances up at him. Nick never returned his look, but stumped on, his boots sparking now and then where the cobbles were dry. He took him through the narrow, dark alleys that threaded backward and forward between wharves. Rats scuttled away from them. Skinny dogs started up from their sleep and settled down again.

At last they came to a large warehouse with a row of carts lined up outside and BEST COALS OF COCKERILL AND CO. painted on them, the letters gleaming white out of the gloom. A man was leading a cart horse out of a barn, and grunted to Nick.

"Thought you weren't coming no more," he said, his voice still hollow with sleep.

"Damn you," said Grimy Nick. "You'd think the worst of the angel Gabriel, you would."

He took Jim around to the front of the warehouse, where it overhung the river, and jumped onto the deck of a lighter that was moored there. It was a flat-nosed boat about eighty feet long. Jim had seen plenty of them working their way backward and forward with the tide, loaded up with tons of cargo from the big ships. It had the name *Lily* painted on its side. It lay in the mud, deep in the stench of the raw sewage that piled against the banks at low tide.

"Get on," Nick growled, and Jim jumped onto the narrow coaming boards that ran around the side of the boat, and looked down into it. Covering one end were planks of wood used for hatch boards, and across these was a long oar. Swinging from the oar was a lantern, casting a dim light into the huge hold, which was piled high with coal. A large, yellow-eyed dog rose on its haunches as soon as Jim jumped onto the hatch, squaring itself to leap. A deep growl rumbled from it, and its teeth shone wet. Jim started back from it. Nick swung around, took him by the shoulders, and pushed him facedown toward the dog. He could smell its sour breath. The dog flattened its ears back and whined.

Nick let go of Jim. "Now he's smelled yer, he'll never forget yer," he said. "Never. He'll know you belong on here, see?"

"Yes," whispered Jim.

"Which means," said Nick, "that if yer tries to run away, he'll be after yer, and he'll prob'ly eat yer alive. The faster yer runs, the faster he runs. See?"

Jim nodded again.

"So yer'd better not try. Just let him taste yer, to sharpen his smell." He pushed Jim's arm down toward the dog. "Bite!"

The dog snapped his jaw so his teeth rested around Jim's wrist. He would have sunk his teeth right in if Jim hadn't held himself steady, though every nerve in him was screaming out.

"Leave!" Nick said, and the dog sank back onto his haunches again, snarling. Jim nursed his arm. The teeth had just punctured the skin, and little points of blood were oozing there.

"He's quite friendly," Nick said. "Just so long as you're friendly to me. See?"

Jim nodded. He was too afraid to speak.

"Well, we'll get along very well, in that case," Nick said. He straightened himself up, took hold of his lantern, and held it up, swinging it slowly from side to side. High up in Cockerill's warehouse, a shutter opened and a white face peered out.

"Don't tell me you're ready!" the white face shouted.

"If we don't get this load out, we'll have lost tomorrow's tide as well as today's."

"I knows that," Nick shouted back. "I've been training my new boy."

The white face disappeared, and a door opened next to the window. A large wicker basket roped to a winch was lowered slowly down, creaking as it came. Nick jumped down into the hold, on top of the coals.

"Lantern," he grunted, and Jim passed it down to him. "Well, get in."

Jim scrambled down beside him, his feet slipping on lumps of coal as he landed. The inside of the lighter was like a black cave, gleaming with heaps of coal. It smelled of damp and sulfur. Nick thrust a shovel at Jim. The basket hovered just above the hold, and Nick eased it down, steadied it, and started shoveling coal into it, his body swinging into a deep, easy rhythm. Jim stabbed at the coals with his shovel. He had to lift it nearly as high as himself before he could tip it into the basket, and the few coals he managed to lift slid off and bumped against him. He gave a little yelp of pain, and Nick stopped shoveling for a moment. He whistled in contempt.

"Get on with it!" he shouted.

Jim panted, trying to slide his shovel under the lumps of coal again, and Nick threw his down and swore at him. He banged his hand across the back of Jim's head and came to stand behind him, reaching around Jim so that his hands were gripping the haft just above Jim's own, forcing Jim to swing into his own level rhythm of shoveling and lifting, shoveling and lifting. When he let go, Jim's hands were burning. Jim did his best to keep up, lifting just two or three coals at a time to Nick's shovelful, bending and lifting, bending and lifting, as if this were all there was to do in the world.

At last the basket was full. Nick yelled up to White-face, and the bucket creaked away from them as it was winched upon its rope to the top story of the building.

Nick swung himself up onto the hatch boards, and somehow Jim pulled himself up after him, rolling well away from the dog. Day had come, gray as pigeons.

The man picked up a pail and emptied water out of it into a cooking pot on a small iron stove. "Get some more," he said to Jim. "There's a pump in the yard."

As Jim jumped across to the planks of the landing stage, he heard Nick say to the dog, "Watch him, Snipe." The dog loped after him, skulking around his legs as he ran, nipping his ankles.

From the back of the warehouse Jim could hear the rumble of the coals as they slid down a chute and onto a waiting cart. The empty basket creaked down again toward the *Lily*.

Jim pumped water into the pail and ran as steadily as he could back to the lighter, the water slopping out against his legs as Snipe nosed against him. Nick had lit a fire in the stove, and he poured some of the water onto a mess of gruel in the cooking pot.

"Stir that," he said to Jim. "And don't take all day."

Jim watched over the gruel until it was beginning to thicken, then lowered himself down into the hold again and swung painfully back into Nick's rhythm. His stomach was beginning to growl with hunger. When the next basket was full, they went back up, and Nick ladled the gruel into two bowls. They ate it fast, squatting on their haunches by the heat of the stove, and when the basket was lowered down again, they left their bowls and set back to work.

They spent the entire day shoveling coal in this way—tons and tons of it. From time to time the white face would appear at the window and shout down to them that the cart was full and that they would have to wait for another. At these times they both stretched themselves full length on the hatch boards of the *Lily*, cold though they were. Jim would fall asleep immediately and would be kicked awake by Nick, or roused by a shout from White-face that the basket was coming down again. His bones seemed to set while he slept. He could hardly kneel or stand, but he was so afraid of Nick and of the yellow-eyed dog that he lumbered up like an old man and hobbled to his job.

A long time after dark, White-face shouted down that he was going home and they could finish for the day. Jim could hardly crawl by then. His shoulders felt as if they had knots of pain in them that would never undo.

Nick put some potatoes in the pot and passed Jim some water to drink. He gurgled it down, his throat dry and parched with coal dust, and dozed off again until the potatoes were ready. He ate his clutched in his palm, burning his skin, peeling it with his teeth the way Nick did. He was glad of it, and of the heat from the fire. He saw that Nick ate meat with his potato and that he tossed what he didn't want of it to Snipe. During the entire day, he had only spoken about a dozen words to Jim.

When he had finished his meal, Nick belched loudly and climbed off the lighter onto the plankway. Jim could hear him trudging past the warehouse and up the alley, and guessed he would be making for one of the alehouses behind the wharf. He was glad. All he wanted now was to go to sleep.

There was a wooden locker with two benches, and he guessed that these were to lie on. He rolled himself up in his sacking. He was so tired that he fell asleep at once. Somehow through his sleep he heard Nick coming back, full of ale and good cheer, saw him tousling Snipe's head and slipping him more meat from his pocket. He didn't take the bench next to Jim, but lowered himself down into the hold of the lighter, and Jim was glad of that, too.

Far out on the river, tugboats hooted. Beside Jim, the yellow dog snuffled into its paws and groaned.

When Jim fell asleep again, he dreamed of his first home, the cottage. Only it was made of coal, its walls and floors and ceilings black and gleaming, reflecting the orange glow of the brazier. On each side of it his mother and father sat with their hands stretched over the fire for warmth. His mother was just as he remembered her: pale and quiet, her dark hair smoothed back. But his father, whose face he never saw in his dreams, looked just like Grimy Nick. He had a gap between his teeth and a frothy beard and gray, thatchy hair, and his face was black with coal dust, his eyes white rings like lights. Jim didn't mind, in his dream, because it looked like a proper home, even though it was made of coal. And it had a name, he was sure of that. It was called the *Lily*.

14

The Waterman's Arms

Jim woke up before Grimy Nick. The river was overflowing with mist and seemed to be breathing with secrets, with dark, looming shapes. When the mist began to lift, they bloomed into life, like a city with street upon street of boats. He could see downriver to the long silver gleam of water, under the dark arches of a bridge, and he knew that far away from there it flowed out to the sea. He imagined slipping the knot of the *Lily* and drifting downstream with her past all the floating castles of tall sailing ships and out to the huge ocean.

When Grimy Nick lumbered up from his dark hole, he swore at Jim for letting the fire in the brazier go out. "You'd think we didn't have any coal on board, you fool." He laughed at his own joke, a great startling whoop of laughter that set Snipe leaping up out of his sleep. Jim tried to laugh with him.

"Get water from the yard," Nick snarled. "Start the day off right."

When Jim came back with his slopping pail, he found Nick toasting fish by the fire. He threw a piece in one direction for Jim and some heads in another direction for the dog. Then he wiped his mouth with the back of his hand and belched.

"Work!" he told Jim. "When we clears this lot, we goes out for more, off one of them big boats. So don't think yer work's done. Yer work's never done. Not while there's coal in the ground."

It took them the whole of that day to clear the hold of coal. Jim thought every bone in his body must break before he'd finished, but Nick kept grimly on, shoveling and lifting and tipping, shoveling and lifting and tipping, his body a grunting shadow swinging across the glow of the lantern. "Work!" Nick shouted at him whenever he paused to rest, swinging his shovel around to crack across the boy's back. Jim struggled to keep up. Sweat poured down him like rain, soaking into him, and when he rubbed his eyes, the grit of coal dust smarted and stung him. By the end of the day he couldn't see what he was lifting or where he was tipping, and no sooner was the basket winched up than he was shoveling coals into empty space, and being shouted at by Nick for his stupidity.

But at last the hold was empty. Nick went up to the desk in the warehouse to get his payment, then came back on board, jingling the coins in his pocket.

"You're only a bundle of sticks," he said to Jim, "but you've worked. If yer wants a bowl of mutton stew, come with me to the alehouse, and I'll see you're set up."

Jim was so tired that he would rather have slept, but he reckoned that Nick's invitation was meant to be some kind of compliment. He didn't dare turn it down. He stumbled after Nick, and the dog loped between them, turning its yellow eyes first to one and then to the other of them.

The Waterman's Arms was dark and noisy, with a low, blackened ceiling and lanterns hanging from the beams. It was thick with smoke from the fire in the hearth and from the men and women who were puffing away at pipes.

Grimy Nick pushed his way toward a crowd of men, who all wore large metal badges on their arms, like him, to show they were watermen. They whistled in contempt when they saw him, but he only laughed in his loud, sharp way. "This is my midget, little Jim, here. Show 'em your muscles, little Jim! Didn't know 'e 'ad any, till he came to work alongside of me." He patted Jim's head in a fatherly sort of way and told him to find a stool by the hearth and to keep quiet.

The barmaid set a bowl of hot stew in front of Jim, and a small draft of ale. He could hardly keep his eyes open now. Before he was halfway through his meal, the noises around him softened out into murmurs and spread across a wide, dark sea, lapping as quiet as long ago. He was slipping into the sea, which wasn't sea at all, but a cradle with soft warm cloths, and it was rocking him as if he were a baby.

There was a crash, and he woke up with a start to find himself lying facedown in the sawdust and his bowl of stew broken and spilled in the hearth. Nick lifted him up and swung him across his shoulders, carried Jim outside past all the laughing, upturned faces, and propped him up on a bench in the dark, with Snipe growling at his feet.

"Wait there," Nick grunted, and went back inside.

Jim was glad to be outside, with the air cold and smarting on his cheeks. He could hear Grimy Nick's voice inside, loud and boastful, and his quick, surprising bellow of laughter. Jim was joined by other children, all squatting or standing in a silent line, waiting for their masters to come out with their food or their pay. Jim puffed himself up a bit. He was the only child there with a beer pot in his hand, even if he did think it tasted like copper coins. He wished he could have his hot mutton stew back.

"You with Grimy Nick?" one boy asked. Jim nodded, taking a quick swig from his pot and scowling at its bitterness.

"His last boy was took to ospickal," the boy muttered. "Beat to bits."

"Won't beat me," said Jim, full of beery bravado. "I'll beat him first."

The other children giggled into their hands at this, turning knowing looks at one another. They were a miserable lot of scarecrows, Jim thought, sipping again at his ale. Some of the children slept where they waited, leaning against each other. One group, roped together, told him they were a field gang, and were waiting to go with their gang leader to dig up turnips on farms.

They were led away at last, and one by one the other children ran off with their coins in their hands. At last Nick came out, breathing bad temper into the cold night.

"Jim, you bag of bones, it's time for you to take me home," he bellowed, as if Jim were two miles away instead of standing beside him, and he leaned his weight on Jim's shoulder. Together they made their slow way to where the *Lily* was moored. Nick stumbled down to his gritty bed in the hold and snored like a foghorn all night.

It seemed as if Jim had only just gone to sleep when he was kicked awake again. Nick, yawning and coughing, pulled him to his feet.

"Move!" he shouted. "Tide's turning!"

Jim staggered up. A fluttering of excitement lit up like a small candle flame inside him. It was time for them to move downstream. Beneath his feet the *Lily* was rocking around, soft as breaths. Jim ran to the wharf and fetched water, and Nick knocked on the door of a nearby cottage and came back with hot bread wrapped in a cloth. By this time the tide was streaming underneath the boat. She nudged around to face downstream, and Nick threw her rope on deck and jumped on board. Jim's dream had come true. They were heading toward the sea.

15

Josh

Grimy Nick stood with his long oar dipping into the water and guided the *Lily* out, and along with her came a flock of barges and sailing boats. The watermen shouted abuse at one another, all racing to find work first. To Jim, the *Lily* was like a waterbird edging her quiet way along the brown river. Even Nick's swearing and whistling didn't take away from him the excitement he was feeling. He looked back and saw the city, with its black pall of smoke hung over it, and he saw the arms of the bridges looping across it, and the slow traffic of sailing boats like dark swans. He heard the *sheesh* of water on the sides of the *Lily* and the steady *plash plash* of Nick's long oar and, above him, the heckling of gulls. Nothing—not all the misery of the last year, not the pain of the last two days, not his fear of Grimy Nick and Snipe—could take away from him the thrill of the journey. It felt like a new beginning.

At last they came to where the big ships lay at anchor. They pulled up alongside a huge coal-carrying boat called the *Queen of the North*, and there Nick pulled in his oar, whistling loudly till a rope ladder was dropped down to him. The *Lily* lay bobbing on the water while Grimy Nick shinned up the rope ladder and went on board the big boat. Jim gazed up after him, longing to follow him. Nick shouted down to him to pull back all the hatch boards. A basket brimming with coals swung out from the boom of the *Queen of the North* and was slowly lowered down. Nick shinned down the ladder again and whistled. "Drop!" he yelled, and the basket creaked down. When it reached Nick's grasp, he and Jim swung it around and tipped the contents into the hold of the *Lily*. Jim spluttered in the clouds of black dust.

"That's your job for today, and tomorrow, till we get the hold full," Nick told Jim. "We've got eighty tons to load, and the quicker we gets it done, the quicker we gets back. See we don't lose any coals overboard. And keep the dog out of the way. And keep moving."

They worked through the day and into the night again. They slept till dawn and set to work again, and at last the hold was so full that Nick had to scramble out of it, coughing and spitting out the coal dust he had swallowed. His face was black, and under the blackened jut of his hair, his eyes gleamed with red rims. His lips shone wet and pink when he opened his mouth, and his few teeth were as bright as polished gems.

"Put some hatch boards across," he ordered. "I'm going for some food." He scrambled back up the ladder, hawking up black spittle as he went.

Jim heaved down the hatch boards and lit the stove, squatting by it for warmth. The afternoon wore on into evening, and a gray gloom settled over the sky. The water glowed with the setting sun, and then faded into the dark. One by one the boats around him had their lanterns hung over their sides. It was as if there were hundreds of small fires dancing on the water. Jim guessed that nothing would move now until the next tide.

From the *Queen of the North* came occasional bursts of laughter and shouts of singing. Jim could smell tobacco. He felt quite happy now that the work had stopped and he could rest. Soon, he knew, Grimy Nick would come swearing back down again and shout at him for something, but at least he would be bringing him food. Jim swilled out his mouth with the last of the water. Snipe lay watching him, his ears sharp, mean points of malevolence, his eyes yellow holes of light. Jim gazed out across the black water. He could hear it breathing, like a huge, waiting beast.

"Hey, below!" a voice called down to him.

Jim jumped up. "Who is it?" He held up the lantern and watched as an unfamiliar pair of boots swung down the ladder toward him. Snipe growled, and then settled down again as the owner of the boots jumped onto the lighter and stroked the dog's head.

"Come to see how Benjamin is," the man said, in a strange accent.

"I don't know him," said Jim.

"The other lad that comes with Nick. Big, clumsy lad," the man said.

Jim remembered what a boy had said to him outside the Waterman's Arms. "I think he might be in hospital."

The man whistled. "Well, I'm not surprised. He looked bad last time I saw him. I've been worrying about him. And I'd say it was Nick that got him that way."

"I don't know." Jim was afraid of saying anything in case this was a trick. Nick might be halfway up the ladder there, dangling in the dark and waiting to pounce on him.

"Beats you, too, does he?" the man asked him.

Jim said nothing.

"Think they own you, some of these masters. Think they own you, body and soul. But they don't. Not your soul. Know what your soul is?"

"No, mister," said Jim, though in his head he imagined it to be something white and fluffy, like a small cloud maybe, floating around his body.

"Well, it's like your name. It comes with you when you're born, and it's yours to keep." The man puffed out his lips, as if it had been hard work thinking that out. "And my name's Josh, and I don't mind telling you that for nothing."

Jim was silent. He half wanted to tell this man about Rosie and Shrimps, and how he used to be known as Skipping Jim, but he kept it to himself. He didn't feel much like skipping anymore. He didn't suppose that he would ever again.

Josh settled down next to the brazier of glowing coals and held out his hands over it as if he would be quite pleased to stay there for the night. He told Jim that Nick was fast asleep on the *Queen of the North*.

"He's stuffed his belly so full that he can't stuff any more in it," Josh said. "So don't expect him down for a bit. Not till the tide comes in, I'd say."

"Where does the tide go to?" Jim asked, a bit timid. He was still wary of Josh, but he liked him, he knew that. He'd never known any man like him before, who spoke kindly to small boys.

"Go to?" Josh puffed out his lips again. "Well, it's just there, isn't it? It's pulled over one way, then it's pulled over another, but it just keeps coming in and out, day after day after day, and it always will. Where there isn't land, there's water—lots of it. And you can only see the top of it. There's more of it underneath. Miles and miles of it. Imagine that!"

Jim tried to imagine it, but he was tired and hungry and thinking was difficult. "Do you live in that boat?" he asked Josh.

"No more than I can help. I've got a proper home. As soon as you lighters take our coal off us, we go home. We sail up the coast of England from here, right up to the north. And that's not the end of the sea, you know. If you just stayed on water, you could go right around the world."

"I wish I could do that," Jim said.

Josh laughed. "You're a funny one, you are. What would you want to do that for? It's big and empty, the sea is. Lonely."

"I might find somewhere nice to live."

Josh laughed again and shook his head. "You don't like living here, then?"

"No, mister, I don't. It's cold and it's hard and I don't get enough food." Jim lowered his voice. "And he shouts and screams so much."

"Not much of a life for a boy," Josh agreed. "I've got a little lad like you. I'm glad he's tucked up in bed with his sisters and his mam, and not stuck out here."

Jim riddled the coals in the brazier. He could feel his cheeks blazing hot and his eyes smarting. He had a new idea inside him, a little feverish will o' the wisp idea. He poked the coals again, easing them around to let the ashes sift through the grid.

Josh stood up and stretched. "Well, I'll be getting up on deck for some sleep. We'll be off with tomorrow's tide." He swung himself onto the ladder.

"Josh." Jim's idea burst out of him, taking him by surprise. "Can I come with you?"

Josh looked down at him. His face was in deep shadow. "Come with me?" His voice was soft. "Why?"

Jim lowered his head and shrugged. His cheeks were burning again. He couldn't find his voice properly. "I think it would be better, that's all," he whispered.

"Nothing gets much better," Josh said. "Not till you're dead."

He hauled himself quickly up the rope, whistling tunelessly between his teeth. Jim sat for a long time with his legs crossed and his arms folded across his knees. The moon was out, bright and round as a mocking face, and the river was billowing up to it, and beyond was blackness. There was no other world but the blackened heart of the lighter and his own small bench space. This was his home.

16

Scraps

Jim lay awake listening to the sounds of laughter that floated down from the *Queen of the North*. He felt very lonely. Clouds had thickened, and the sky was darker than he had ever known it. The night seemed to stretch on forever.

I wish I'd got a brother, he thought. He said it out loud. "I wish I'd got a brother." His voice was a tiny, quavering thing. He stood up and shouted. "I wish I'd got a brother!"

He thought of Tip, sleeping in the workhouse in the snuffling darkness. He thought of Shrimps in a lodging house full of snoring old men. He thought of Josh's son, tucked up in a proper bed with a real mother and sisters.

"You got lots of bruvvers, Jim," he said to himself, the way Shrimps would have said it. "Only they ain't around at the moment, is all."

He pulled his sack around him and fell asleep.

* * *

Grimy Nick was laughing softly to himself as he came down the ladder. The sky was the color of milk. Jim started up out of his slumber, his first thoughts to the fire in the brazier, in case he'd let it go out. Nick tossed a bone to the dog, who leaped on it, growling. Jim held out his hands for his food. Nothing.

"There's work to do soon, such as you've never seen before," Nick told him. He half fell down into the hold, sending the packed coals skittling.

Snipe snarled and guzzled over his bone, his paws securing it. Jim could smell the meat on it. Tell him, bruvver, a voice in Jim's head said. He's forgot you. Tell him!

"Nick," Jim whispered.

Nick snorted and turned over.

Hunger gave Jim courage. "Did you forget my food?"

With one rapid movement, Nick tossed away his blanket. He hauled himself up out of the hold and onto the boards.

"Forgot, did I?"

"I think so, Nick."

"Here's food for you." Nick bent down and snatched the bone from the dog's jaws. Snipe's teeth snapped down on it, and Nick kicked him off. He grabbed Jim's hand and thrust the boy's face into the bone so that his mouth was pressed against it. He could smell the dog's breath on it. Jim squirmed to get away. The dog sprang and fixed his teeth around Jim's hand, and as Jim tore it away, Snipe bit again, worrying and snapping, till with a shout of laughter Nick flung the bone across the boards. The dog pounded after it and lay guarding it, growling, his eyes fixed on Jim.

"There's food for you, if you want it," Nick said. He stood with his hands on his hips, watching Jim. The boy sank back on his heels again.

"No time for eating now, nor sleeping." Nick lifted up his head, sniffing the air. "I reckon we've got the tide."

With the hold full of coal, the lighter lumbered slowly back upstream. Nick stood working the oar, staring ahead of him, yelling sometimes to other light-ermen as they drew close. The whole fleet of river craft was moving home at the same time, like flies swarming.

It wasn't until they were in sight of the wharves again, and all the bridges and domes and towers of the city, that Nick leaned around to look at Jim.

"You done all right," he told him, and taking a hand-ful of scraps of meat out of his pocket, he threw them at him, laughing at Jim's surprised face.

But Jim didn't dive for them, as Nick expected. Noth-ing would have tempted him to pick up the meat. He wanted to kick the meat overboard into the river, but he couldn't bring himself to admit that he had even seen it. Better to pretend it wasn't there at all. He turned away, fists clenched, and thought of the big bowl of meat Nick would have eaten on the *Queen of the North*, with gravy and mustard and hot potatoes. He could have called to Jim to come up with him and share it with him. Instead he had shoved the leftovers of his plate into the grimy dust of his pocket. Jim hated him for it. When he turned around again, he saw that the dog had eaten the lot.

You wouldn't have ate it anyway, bruvver, the voice in his head muttered. Would have stuck in your throat.

Nick stood with his hands in his pockets, whistling quietly and watching the dog. "Well, you're an odd one," he said to Jim. "I don't knows if I understands you."

Don't answer him, bruv, Jim thought. If he can't be bovvered to give you proper food, don't you be bovvered to talk, see? Just pretend he ain't there at all.

As soon as the *Lily* had nosed into the wharf outside Cockerill's coal yard, Jim and Nick set to work. White-face lowered down the basket, and they filled it up, watched it being winched up to the chute, waited for it to come down empty again. Jim knew the pattern of his life now: filling up the hold of the *Lily* from the big coal-carrying ships that waited outside the port, bringing it upriver to the warehouse, emptying it so that it could be taken by horse and cart to the people of London. Backward and forward, filling and emptying, shoveling and piling, day after day after day. And never a word spoken between him and Nick. He would sleep on his hard bunk every night of his life. He would eat when Nick thought fit to feed him. He was Nick's slave, and he was treated worse than an animal.

I wish I was Snipe, he thought sometimes when Nick fondled the dog's head and fed him tasty scraps from his pocket.

Once or twice when they moored up to the *Queen of the North* again, Nick showed by a jerk of his head that Jim was to follow him on board. Jim looked around eagerly for Josh, but he never saw him again. "He got a job onshore," one of the men told him. "Wanted to see more of his family. Said he'd met a little boy who made him long to be at home again."

Jim didn't like the rough company of the men as much as he had liked Josh. Their voices were loud and boastful, but at least they were a change from the silent, brooding company of Grimy Nick. And he was sure of food when he went on board. But he never again thought of hiding on deck and sailing off with them. If he did, the men would find him and take him back to Nick; he was sure of that. There was no escape—ever.

But Jim did try to escape one night. He had been living with Nick nearly a year before his chance came.

There was a sudden storm, so wild that they made straight for the riverbank instead of heading back to the wharves. The river rolled and heaved like a boneless beast, tossing the *Lily* as if she were made of matchsticks. Jim clung to the side, weak and afraid, but as soon as they pulled in and tied up to land he felt better. Nick and Snipe settled into sleep.

Jim heard the faint sound of bells. Through the slant of rain he could see a village in the distance, and a church tower. He could run to it for shelter. Maybe the storm was making such a noise that Nick and Snipe wouldn't even hear him going.

Come on, bruvver! the voice in his head urged. You can do it! You can do it!

Jim slid over to the coamings. They were awash with rain. He swung one leg over the edge, then the other, and just as he was about to lever himself up to jump, his arm caught on the oar, which had been propped up across the boat. It slid down with a sickening thud.

Snipe's ears jerked up to listening points. Immediately into the storm were tossed strange pieces of sound: the barking of a dog, the shouting of a man, and the crying of a boy in pain.

"Thought yer'd try it, did yer?" Nick bellowed. He picked Jim up and threw him down into the hold of the *Lily*, on top of the coals. "Yer'll know better next time!" He slid the hatch boards shut over Jim's head.

Jim lay in the dark, nursing his leg where Snipe had ripped his flesh. It was hot and wet with blood. He had never known such pain in his life before.

17

The Monster
Weeps

For several days Jim lay in the hold, too weak to move. His leg hurt so much that he thought he would never walk again. Nick worked around him, watching him and scowling.

"Get up, can't you? Get up!" he shouted at him one day. "I've got something for you, if you get up."

Jim struggled to his feet. He was afraid of what might happen to him if he didn't show that he was willing to work. Nick watched him, whistling.

"Come over here now."

Jim limped across to him, pleased with himself for doing it without letting Nick know how much it hurt. As soon as he reached him, Nick pushed Jim's head down and tied a rope around his neck. He fastened the other end to a hook on the deck board.

"Caught you, my wild bird!" He chuckled. "There'll be no flying away now!"

Jim turned away, saying nothing. I'll get my revenge,

he thought. One day, Nick. You'll be sorry you did this to me.

One summer morning, Jim limped from Cockerill's yard with a brimming pail of water. There was no need these days for Snipe to follow him to the pump yard and back. He would just squat at the gate, watching, his tongue lolling out and his ears up sharp. Even if Jim had managed to untie the rope, he wouldn't have been able to run away from Snipe. It had taken months for the scars in his leg to heal, and even so he couldn't put his weight on it properly.

He lifted the water on board and made porridge, just as he did every morning when they were moored at Cockerill's, while Nick shoveled coal into the basket. When the porridge was ready, he banged his wooden spoon on the cooking pot. He never spoke to Nick these days.

Nick yelled up to White-face to haul up the basket, and as it creaked past him, Jim noticed how frayed the rope had become. The strands were taut and straight instead of twisted into a plait, and even as he watched, one or two of the threads began to snap. Slowly the basket swayed up. Jim stood up, watching it. The hairs on his neck began to tremble, and his heart began to beat a light, rapid rhythm—a dance of warning.

Nick was groping his way slowly out of the hold. High above his bent back, the basket began to tilt.

Then, "Nick!" Jim yelled.

Nick looked up sharply, saw Jim's upturned face, and

flung himself sideways. At that very instant the rope snapped and all the coals rained down.

And then the air settled into a choking silence. Snipe howled, snuffling into the scattered coals. White-face shouted from his top window and came hurrying down the iron stairs of the warehouse, his boots clanging on every step. Jim didn't move from the spot.

White-face shoved past him and stood gazing down at the heap of coals. He ran back and shook Jim into life.

"Don't stand there, boy. Help me."

With his bare hands White-face scrabbled, moaning out loud. Cold and quiet, Jim knelt down beside him. He eased the coals slowly away, picking them out one by one and placing them behind him. He was deeply frightened.

"Look!" he whispered at last, and White-face stopped his scrabbling.

The coals seemed to be stirring of their own accord. It was as if they were breathing. A pair of blackened hands groped through, then a face, blinking into the light, and, like a monster rising from the deep, Grimy Nick emerged. He staggered up, shaking sprays of black dust. Snipe hurled himself against him. Nick crouched down onto the boards again, breathing heavily, staring around him as though he couldn't believe where he was.

"I'll get a doctor for you," White-face said. He was shaking.

"No, yer don't," Nick snarled. "I can't afford a doctor. I'll live."

"And you can thank your boy for that," White-face told him. He scrambled back onto the landing stage, checking the time on his pocket watch. "I reckon he saved your life." He clanged back up the stairs, counting them out loud as he went.

Jim couldn't bear to look at Nick. It wasn't that he was afraid of him. He would never be afraid of him again now, he knew that. But what he couldn't bear was the noise that was coming from him—little whimpers, bubbling up out of him, blubbers of sound—and when he looked, he saw white trails running down Nick's cheeks, coursing through the coal dust, filling up and coursing through again, as if they would never stop.

18

You Can Do It, Bruvver

It was autumn. A washing tub drawn by six geese led the procession on the river. Men swam behind it. All the barges and lighters were decorated with flags and flowers and white rags that fluttered like the feathers of swans. Some of the men were being rolled down the river, in barrels, to hoots of laughter. The banks were lined with watchers, all dressed in bright rags and shiny coats, playing bugles and beating drums. A family of beggars was singing hymns, and the tiny voices of the children piped like birds. It was the miners' pageant, and the *Lily* drifted along in the procession, freed from work for the day. Nick and his fellows shouted to one another and sang.

Drawn up among the watching people were some painted wagons. Two clowns stood with mournful faces, holding up a green-and-crimson banner. "Juglini's Champion Circus," Nick read out.

What's a circus? Jim wanted to ask, but wouldn't. The showman's family came out of their wagon to watch.

The man and the woman each carried a child, and older children danced around them. A boy of Jim's age did a handstand and waggled his feet at the barges. Jim waved to him, and the boy dropped down, waved, and swung up again.

See, the voice in his head said. Another bruvver, Jim. They're all over the place, ain't they?

For a time, as the procession sailed past, the circus boy ran alongside the *Lily*, waving and shouting, "Come to the circus! Come to the circus!" Then he fell back as the crowd became thicker.

Jim cupped his hands around his mouth. "I will! I will!" he shouted back. They were nearing another village. Jim stood up and strained to keep the boy in sight. He could hear the circus band, the roll of drums, the tooting of trumpets and trombones. He imagined he could still hear the boy's voice.

The main point of the pageant seemed to be for the coalmen and lightermen to pull up at every village and visit the local alehouse and get as drunk as possible on their pageant money. Grimy Nick lurched and stumbled with the rest of them, and his singing became louder and more slurred. He stowed his long oar inside the hold and laughed down at Jim's excited face.

"Want to go pageanting, do you?"

"Please, Nick. . . . Can I?"

Nick whistled in his scornful way and stumped off. Jim watched him go, hating him. He crouched down by Snipe, fingering the rope around his neck. Night was settling down on the water, though it was still warm. Families were gathered on the banks, and children were being called together by their mothers. They eyed him curiously as they went past and whispered to one another, their hands across their mouths. Jim knew they were laughing at him.

What are you doing here, the voice in his head asked him, tied up like an animal, eating and sleeping like an animal, no one to talk to? Time you went. Time you skipped away, bruvver, and no mistake.

He stood up, and Snipe snarled at him. Jim thought about his lucky chance at the workhouse when he had decided to escape with the carpets—how he had leaped at it, how well it had worked. If he had managed that time, he'd manage again. His last attempt had been reckless; he'd jumped without thinking. He would be mad to think of taking a chance like that again. But this time his thoughts were calm and steady. He wasn't going to leap at anything. But he was going to get away. He knew that.

By the time the night was out, he knew, Grimy Nick would be drunker than he'd ever been before. It was Jim's perfect chance. He knew exactly what to do.

While he waited, he lowered himself down into the hold and found some big heavy chunks of coal. He carried them up onto the boards and hid them. Then he found a small, sharp piece. He ran his hand along the edge of it. Just right.

He laid the boards down across the coamings till they covered the hold completely, except for the small hatch board. Then he took the piece of sharp coal and rubbed it against the rope that was around his neck. It seemed to take hours. His wrist was aching. He thought the rope would never begin to fray, but all at once he felt the strands fluffing up and beginning to weaken. If Nick came while he was doing it, he thought, he would just put his head down and pretend to sleep. It was only a matter of time now. The rope had to give. Bursts of sound erupted on the river and in the village. Jim worked on, scraping and scraping at the rope. It had to give.

At last he was through. The last slice of the coal cut his neck as the final strand snapped, but he didn't care. He held the frayed end in his hand and edged up to Snipe, careful not to startle him. The dog opened his yellow eyes and growled.

"It's all right, Snipe. It's all right."

He forced himself to stroke the dog's matted fur. Again Snipe growled. Jim kept on stroking him and talking to him softly, all the time listening out for Grimy Nick. At last he judged the dog to be calm enough. He slipped the rope around Snipe's neck and secured it. Good.

Then he heard Nick coming back, singing and stumbling along the riverbank. It didn't matter. Jim had a plan for that. When Nick lumbered on deck, he raised the lantern and saw his boy and his dog sleeping side by side, the boy with his hand on the dog's neck. He was touched by their peacefulness. He tried to creep past them, lost his footing, and tumbled into his hold. Jim and Snipe both strained their ears, listening. Almost at once Nick's breathing steadied into a rumbling snore.

For a long time Jim waited. Onshore, all the voices had quieted down. The hens and dogs, the cows and pigs in all the backyards of all the villages, had settled in for the night.

Jim stirred slowly. Snipe half woke. Jim sat for a bit and then sidled his way to the hold. He watched the dog till it sank its head back into its paws.

Come on. You can do it, bruvver. You can.

And he knew that he could.

Slowly, slowly, he stood up, took hold of the hatch cover, and lowered it down. The dog slept on. One by one, and taking what seemed to be an eternity over it, he lifted up the big chunks of coal that he had brought up earlier and, without making a sound, placed them on the hatch. He worked slowly and steadily, and still the dog slept. Then he straightened himself up. Nothing moved. Not a sound.

He crept over to the side of the deck, glanced quickly around at the dog, and with one swift movement rolled himself off the lighter and onto the bank. He righted himself and began to run.

19

Away

Instantly Snipe was awake. His howls rang across the night. He strained to pull against the rope, in a fury to be free. Grimy Nick hollered himself into wakefulness and pummeled his fists against the hatch. Across the fields, all the backyard animals sent up their clamor. Lights blazed across the water.

Jim sprinted on steadily, head down, dodging between bushes and trees. He could hear his own breathing and the flapping of his boot soles. Brambles tore at his breeches and his jacket. An overhanging branch snapped at his cap and held it trapped, and Jim had to run back and tear it free. He loped on, his chest tight and bursting, his legs as heavy as lead weights. He had no idea where he was going.

He heard rustling in the undergrowth behind him and knew that he was being followed. The rustling became a snuffling and panting. A dog. Jim's leg hurt so much now that he couldn't run any farther. In total weariness, he flung himself down, headfirst, covered his face with his hands, and waited for Snipe to spring.

He was aware that everything had gone silent again, as if the world had sunk back into sleep. At last he made himself turn his head. The dog was not Snipe at all, but a small terrier. He licked Jim's outstretched hand and ran away again through a hedge. There wasn't a sound. If Snipe still howled, he couldn't be heard from here. If Nick still hammered and swore, then the noise he made was lost in the night.

What if they're dead, bruvver? the voice crept into his head. What if old Nick's smothering down there in the hold? What if Snipe's strangled himself on that rope? He sat up, drenched with cold sweat. What if you've killed them?

He trusted himself to stand up. There wasn't a sound. He whistled softly for the dog, who padded back through the hedge to him, ran up, and then danced away. He was alone again, and this time it was the silence that made him afraid. He crawled into the hedge, hoping to sleep, but the silence boomed around him.

Now you've done it, the little voice whispered. You've left your master to smother, and you've strangled his dog on the rope. You've killed them both, you have. Now you're in for it, Jim.

20

The Green
Caravan

Jim woke to the sound of horses, a thudding of
hooves that made the earth shake. He ran to the
edge of his field and scrambled through the thickness
of trees till he came to a wide clearing in another field.
There must have been twenty or more horses being
exercised, all in a ring. In the center of the ring a man
stood with a whip, lashing the ground with it and
shouting out commands that made the horses stop, rear,
turn, and trot in the other direction. They were nothing
like the workhorses that Jim had seen pulling carriages,
or Lame Betsy's bony old knock-kneed dairy horse.
These horses were powerful and lively, high-stepping
like dancers.

At the other end of the field was a monster tent.
Men and children were shouting and laughing out loud,
hauling on the ropes to pull it upright. The tent was
like a huge green bird that wouldn't lie still. And all
around the sides of the field were caravans, all painted
with bright colors.

The biggest of them had words painted on them, and Jim knew for sure that they would say JUGLINI'S CHAMPION CIRCUS. One wagon had a green door with a brass knocker and cabin windows with muslin curtains and a funnel at the back with smoke curling from it. From the back window a woman gazed out at him, as if she was daydreaming, not really noticing him at all. Jim guessed that this would be Madame Juglini herself. He remembered how her children had danced and waved to him from the riverbank, and instinctively he put up his hand to feel for the rope that had tied him around the neck. But he was free of that—forever, he hoped.

A wonderful smell of cooking arose from the caravan. Jim couldn't remember when he had last eaten. Whenever it was, it had only been the scraps from Grimy Nick's pockets.

As Jim watched, the woman disappeared and was replaced by two small children. Jim recognized them as the two younger ones he'd seen on their parents' shoulders the day before. They caught sight of him and pointed at him, laughing.

The woman opened the door of the wagon. Her children squirmed onto the step in front of her and giggled at Jim.

"Please, ma'am . . . ," Jim began. If he hadn't been so hungry, he would have run back into the trees to hide, but the smell of food was stronger and sweeter than ever.

He waved his hands to where the men were heaving and straining at the tent ropes. "I've come for a job if you'll give me one," he faltered.

Memories of Nick came floating up to him. What have I done? he thought. What's happened to Nick? Immediately, hunger chased the thoughts away. Eat first, and then think. That was best.

"I'll help to put the tent up. I'll muck out the horses, and clean 'em up bright and smart. And I don't want money, missus."

"Don't want money?" Madame Juglini frowned down at him. "I've never heard that before."

"If you'll feed me, missus," Jim said, all his confidence gone, "I'll do anything."

He gazed at the little wagon, and his old longing rose up in him again. How good it must be to live in this green van with the shining brass knocker on the door and the chimney curling out smoke. He dug his hands deep into his pockets. There was nothing more he could say.

A boy came running across the field to the caravan. He stopped short, staring at Jim.

Madame Juglini went back up the steps. "Antonio, you bring the boy inside."

Jim followed the boy Antonio into the caravan and gazed around at the bright cushions and curtains, at the small fire crackling in its burner, and at all the neat, shiny fittings. He had never seen anything that looked so much like a home. He was conscious now of his filthy hands and broken, blackened nails, and of the tattered state of his clothes.

Madame Juglini gave him some food and watched him while he ate. She knew the white marks around his eyes for what they were. She sighed. "We have a busy day. We have a costume to make for the Strongest Man in the Universe. The last Strongest Man ran away with a Flying Lady and took his loincloth with him." Her children giggled. "You don't sew, I suppose?" she asked Jim.

Jim could have told her about the weeks he'd spent making sacks in the workhouse, but he didn't dare, in case it was a trick question. He shrugged. "I might be able to," he said. The small children laughed at him.

Mr. Juglini came in, rubbing his hands together, and tousled Jim's hair as if he were quite used to seeing him sitting at his table. A cloud of black dust rose from Jim's head, and Antonio pretended to dodge away from him, coughing.

"This boy says he wants a job," his wife said.

Mr. Juglini sat down opposite Jim and stared at him. Then he leaned toward him.

"Now tell me true," he began. "Have you run away from home?" His black eyes seemed to burn right into Jim's.

Jim felt the scorch of tears, and tried to rub them away. "I used to live on a coal lighter," he said. "I . . . I think the lighterman might have died, sir. I think he might have got trapped. It was . . . I . . . did . . ."

Madame Juglini and her husband exchanged glances.

"He can whiten the harnesses with Antonio. There's a job. Let's see how well he does it." Juglini smoothed his mustache and went quickly out of the wagon.

Jim gazed after him, so many words tumbling about in his head that he couldn't find a single one to say.

21

Circus Boy

By midday the huge tent was up, and sawdust had been scattered in its ring. Madame Juglini was away for most of the day, but came back at dusk, just as the lanterns were lit around the field, hanging from trees like ripe orange fruit. The tent glowed with yellow gaslight.

Jim and Antonio stood by the gates of the field beating drums, and the circus band paraded around the tent, bugles and trumpets blaring into the twilight. Bats skittered over their heads like black rags.

Up the lane came a rumble of wheels, and the children of the circus cheered. "The people are coming, the people are coming!" At the door flap of the tent, Madame Juglini was taking money and shouting, "Roll up! Roll up, for the greatest show on earth! See the Flying Horses of Arabie! See Madame Bombadini as she flies through the air! See the Strongest Man in the Universe!"

Jim and Antonio ran inside the tent and wriggled

underneath the tiers of benches. They squatted there, arms folded, beneath the drumming feet of the impatient audience. Bits of orange peel and nutshells showered down on them. Antonio smiled at Jim.

It would be all right now. Everything would be all right. Tonight Jim would sleep in the green caravan with the brass door knocker, and tomorrow he would help to take down the big tent with the men and the children. He would march in the procession with his drum. Roll up! Roll up! He closed his eyes, letting the music and the voices swirl around him.

Antonio nudged him. The drums started up a booming roll. The crowd roared. Mr. Juglini ran into the ring and cracked his whip for silence. The band blazed, and into the ring ran the horses—the beautiful, powerful horses, scudding and shining—the thundering, billowing horses. Juglini cracked his whip again, and the horses reared onto their back legs, and into their circle another horse galloped, with a woman standing on the saddle, her muslin skirts tucked up high. As the crowd cheered, she leaned right back, her arms outstretched, and somersaulted. "One, two, three!" Juglini shouted.

"Four! Five! Six!" the crowd roared. Over she went, and over again, and came up each time smiling and proud. Jim cheered and clapped. He wanted to stand up and shout, "Hooray for Juglini's circus!"

It was then, as the horses turned with a swish of their tails and a prancing of their long legs, that Jim saw what he had never thought to see again in his life. The entrance flap of the tent was lifted up briefly. He could just make out the face of Madame Juglini, peering and anxious. He saw her hand, stretched up to receive a coin. And next to hers, like a specter, another face, looming in the glow of the lantern: a square, blackened face, with hair like a slipping thatch, and eyes that bulged through like lamps.

22

On the Run Again

Far away behind him Jim could hear the beating of the drums and the blare of the trumpets and trombones, the roar of the crowd. When he paused to look around, he could see the glow of the huge tent and the dark shapes of the caravans parked around the edges of the field. He could just make out which one was Juglini's.

He turned away again and ran until he could run no more. He reached a barn near a farmhouse. The door was open. He crept in and curled himself up in a pile of straw. His last thoughts, as sleep overtook him, were of something that Shrimps had said long ago: "I'd rather sleep in a barn full of rats, and I done that a time or two."

Jim listened to the scurryings around him. Well, he thought, rats is charming company, bruvver. At least they knows where it's warm and dry.

The cry of the farmyard cockerel woke him up, and the sun striping through the barn roof. Jim lay still and tense, listening to the sound of the farmworkers making their way to the fields. When their voices had died away, he left the barn. Hens cluttered around him and squawked away again.

An old woman, swaying as she walked, came out of the farm building, carrying two large pails. She swayed past the barn where Jim crouched, afraid, her skirts sweeping up the hens' grain as they bobbed around her. She went into the milking shed. Jim could hear her talking to the cows, and the low muttering the beasts made.

He dared himself to creep out of the barn again. The old woman had left the kitchen door open. Jim peered in. He could see bread on the table—left over from the men's breakfast—pies and cheeses, a big jug of milk. Maybe if he asked the woman, she would give him food. Maybe she would shut him into a back room and go and fetch Grimy Nick. He didn't feel he could ever trust anyone again.

He glanced around the yard and sneaked into the kitchen, stuffing as much food as he could into his mouth, cramming his pockets till they bulged. He heard a creak on the stair, swigged from the jug, grabbed one last desperate handful of cheese, and turned to see a girl on the middle step, her hand to her mouth.

He dropped the jug and ran. The girl followed him, shouting, the jug clattering still on the flagged floor. The old woman hurried out of her milking shed, and all the farm dogs barked. Jim was away like a hare before a hound, streaking up to the lane.

He had no idea, now, where he was. The river was a long way away, and he could no longer see any signs of villages. A stagecoach rumbled past, and he flung himself into the trees, turning his face away from the dust and the staring eyes of the passengers. What if one of them was Grimy Nick, glittering with revenge?

He limped steadily on. His leg hurt a lot now. He passed a family of beggars, trudging in their bare feet, bundles on their backs.

"At least you don't have to carry anything," he said to himself. "You count yourself lucky, bruvver."

His boots flapped as he walked. The nails had worked their way out and the soles were like lolloping tongues.

"Chuck them in a ditch," he told himself, but he knew he couldn't do that. They were Lizzie's boots, from long ago. They were the only things he had to call his own, besides his name. He shoved one into each pocket. Now he couldn't even hear his own footsteps. Every now and again a lapwing squeaked in a plowed field, or a small animal rustled the hedgerow leaves, startling him. He seemed to be walking forever along the silent lanes, with the huge gray sky arching over him. He was tense with listening. He imagined he saw Grimy Nick lurking behind every tree, his shadow flittering every time he turned around, his thin, mocking whistle piercing through every bird song.

"Keep going, bruvver," he urged himself. "This must lead somewhere."

At last he came to a signpost. It was a magic thing,

he felt. He traced the letters with his fingers, one by one. " 'London Town.' It *has* to be," he said.

"You're going home!" he whispered. "Rosie lives in London Town, Jim!" Home. He ate some food under his magic signpost and set off again, faster this time. The sun was setting low and red across the fields, but the air was becoming hazier and sootier. London was near.

23

Shrimps Again

Everything was growing familiar, yet everything was wrong. He was near the river, near the wharves and the warehouses, but the houses were gone. Everywhere he looked, men were hammering and digging, lifting loads of rubble onto carts, heaving great planks of wood down to the water's edge. Skeletons of houses crumbled into piles of dust. And Rosie's cottage, and the boat shed where he had first watched the river, had gone.

Jim stared in disbelief at the wreckage around him. It looked as if the whole city was being destroyed in order to build a new one.

"What's happening?" he asked someone, a woman who reminded him of Rosie, with fat arms and a brown shawl wrapped over her head and shoulders.

"They're building a big new dock here, for all the boats," she told him, never taking her eyes off the workmen. "Wunnerful, ain't it! Wunnerful. They say there's more than two thousand men working here.

Fancy! I never knew there was two thousand men in the whole world!" She laughed, a coarse, grating laugh.

"But what happened to all the houses?" Jim asked her. "And all the people who lived here? Where's Rosie?"

The woman laughed again and rubbed her arms. "Rosie? I know a dozen Rosies, and they've all lost their homes now. Don't know where any of the Rosies have gone. Pastures new, I hope!"

Jim wandered away from her. She was so fascinated by the builders that she would stand and watch all day, no doubt of it, her fat arms folded with patient curiosity, her weight shifting from one leg to the other.

You're on your own now, bruvver, and no mistake. You ain't got no one.

Nothing was familiar to Jim anymore. He'd lost his bearings. He'd been so used to the slow journey of the *Lily* and the silent company of Grimy Nick that he'd forgotten what it was like to be in the city with its mucky streets and the constant push and stench of the crowds. He wandered around, hoping in vain to see Rosie. He did see one woman selling seafood, and he ran up to her to ask her if he could help.

"Help me?" She laughed down at him. "What can you do to help me, little chap?"

"I could dance for you, and shout out, 'Shrimpso! Whelkso!'" he told her. "It would bring all the people around to buy from you. I used to do it for Rosie."

"And as soon as they come, you'd pick their pockets and we'd both be done for it," the woman said. "Not likely. Clear off."

Jim moved away from her. Then he started to skip—
glancing at her to make sure she was watching—a little,
helpless dance. He was sad and tired and hungry. He
didn't feel like skipping at all. His leg hurt. He felt
wretched, deep inside himself, black with wretch-
edness. The woman shook her head at him and walked
away

"Give us some shrimps, lady?" the street boys called
after her in their whining voices. She ignored them.

Jim sank down onto his heels. One of the boys hun-
kered down next to him.

"You remind me of Skippin' Jim," he said. "He used
to come round 'ere."

Jim looked at him. "You don't know a boy called
Shrimps, do you?"

" 'Course I do!" The boy laughed "Everyone knows
Shrimps."

"Know where he is?" Jim asked.

The boy jumped up and darted off, and Jim followed
as best as he could, dodging between barrows and stalls
right around the back of the marketplace. It was dusk,
and the stalls had their red wax candles glowing among
their fruits and fishes. The little boy snatched at some
apples on his way past one stall, and so did Jim. They
grabbed cheeses and pies, and the child took off his
cap and stuffed it full with his takings. Jim's spirits were
up. He could hardly believe he was really going to see
Shrimps again, after all this time. He knew for sure, as
he ran along, that the voice that had been in his head
all these months had been Shrimps's.

Wait till I tell you everything I've done, bruvver! he thought as he ran. Make your ears tingle, it will.

At the back of the market there were some piled-up wooden crates that had held tea from India and spices from Zanzibar, and the little boy wriggled his way through them. He stopped by an upturned crate that was filled with straw. Lying on top of the straw, deep in the shadows, was a thin, pale ghost of a boy, a bundle of bones dressed in dirty rags.

"Here's Shrimps," the child told Jim. "Only he's badly now. Awful badly."

He emptied his cap of the stolen food. "Here y'are, Shrimps," he said. "Some bits to eat and that, like I promised. Only I can't stop; there's work to do. But someone's come to see you." He motioned to Jim to take his place, and ran off again.

Jim crawled between the crates.

"Shrimps?" Jim said. He felt awkward and shy. "It's Skipping Jim. Remember?" The boy didn't answer. Jim could hear the rasping of his breath.

"You all right?" He could hardly see him, except for the orange tufts of his hair sticking up above his white face. His fingers fluttered like pale moths, edging and fumbling as he pulled his sack toward his face. Jim knelt down and broke open an orange with his thumbs, squeezing the juice into Shrimps's mouth.

"When you're better," he said, "we'll go round together, like you said."

He kept his voice bright, but inside he was deeply afraid. He sat for a long time listening to the way

Shrimps's breath rasped and shivered in his throat. The market sounds clamored into the night, and long before they died down, Jim crawled into the tea chest next to Shrimps to try to keep him warm.

24

Looking for a
Doctor

Next morning Jim searched around for sacking and straw to help to make Shrimps more comfortable. He managed to prop him up so that he could eat more easily. But the boy only pecked at food.

"Shrimps," said Jim, uneasy, "what's up with you?"

"Old age, bruvver."

In his heart Jim was afraid it might be the cholera. Many people were dying of that, he knew.

"What really happened, Shrimps?"

"I got beat up, didn't I? This old gentleman give me a guinea, honest he did. Prob'ly thought it was a farthing, but he give me a guinea, fair and square. I think he took a fancy to me charming face."

"I believe you."

"And I was follered down this alley. Some blokes said I'd nicked it off the old gentleman and I had to give it back. And when I said I hadn't, they started kicking me and punching me like I was a rag doll. But I wasn't going to give me guinea up, was I? It was a present.

Sooner give it to me ma than to them blokes. So I stuck it under me armpit. Anyway, they must've knocked me out good and proper. When I came to, me jacket had gone and me guinea wiv it, and all me laces, too. So the lads brought me here. Carried me, they did."

"You should be in the hospital."

Shrimps panicked then. "I don't want no ospickal. I don't want no ospickal." He was so scared that he tried to scramble out of the crate, knocking over the pot of water Jim had brought for him.

"I won't take you there," Jim promised him. "Not if you don't want to go."

Soon Shrimps drifted off to sleep. It frightened Jim, watching him. It reminded him of the way his mother had been. He was afraid to leave him, and he was afraid to stay with him. When Shrimps woke again, he coughed as if his body would break in half. He leaned back after the fit, exhausted.

"Fink I swallowed a fly, Jim," he said. "Must've slept wiv me mouth open."

As he was drifting back to sleep again, Jim told him about Rosie's grandfather and about Grimy Nick and Snipe. He told him about the terrible night when he thought he'd murdered Grimy Nick, and about the circus, and about Grimy Nick's appearance in the big tent.

"Ghosts is s'posed to be white and thin, not coalie-black wiv eyes like fires." Shrimps chuckled.

When Shrimps slept again, Jim went off in search of food and help. One stallholder threw a cabbage at him, and he caught it before it hit him. "Thanks, mister!" he shouted. He ran back to the crates with it, broke up some boxes for firewood, and that night he begged a light from the night watchman. He ran back to the crates with his flare blazing and cooked the cabbage in the water pot over the fire. He ate well that night, and even Shrimps managed to swallow some of the soupy liquid.

"That was a feast, Jim," he said, belching softly and lying back. His face in the firelight was full of deep shadows. "I'll be better soon."

But Shrimps didn't get better. He had been starving for too long. Jim didn't know what to do to help him. He brought him fresh straw to lie on, but it was all he could do to roll him over and stuff it underneath him.

Shrimps was afraid that their hiding place would be found by the police. He made Jim pile up more and more boxes around them. The nights were bitterly cold, and the sun was so weak that the daytime was hardly warmer. Winter was upon them.

Jim had asked all the fruit-and-vegetable sellers at the market for help. Some of the women came to peer at Shrimps in his crate, but they'd seen many a child in that state before, and they just shrugged. The street boys brought him things to eat, but he was too ill to touch them.

"Needs a doctor, he does," one of the women said.

"He can't go to the hospital. I promised him," Jim said. He was desperate for help. Didn't anybody care? "He's scared of being taken to the workhouse."

The woman nodded "Nowhere else for him," she said, turning her back on the crate, rubbing her arms for warmth. " 'Cept a pauper's grave, and that'll be a blessing." She was already walking away as she said it.

Jim tried begging for money. He waited outside the theaters where Shrimps used to sell his laces to the rich people. "Please," he would say to the ladies and gentlemen stepping out of their carriages, "my brother's ever so ill. Please can I have some money for a doctor?" But they would turn away as if they hadn't really seen him.

When he went back to Shrimps, he didn't even try to get him to eat. He just moistened his lips with water. Shrimps's eyes flickered open.

"Lovely bit of beer, that is," he whispered, and fell asleep again.

One night Jim went to the theater queue again, but this time he didn't ask for money. He skipped for them instead, and when they saw that he wasn't holding his cap out for coins, and how lightly he danced, they started to take notice of him. Through the ragged holes in his trousers they could see the deep scar on his leg, but he danced as well as he had ever done. When quite a few people were gathered around him, he stopped and clapped his hands.

"Can anyone give me the name of a doctor, please?" he shouted. "One that won't charge money?"

Nobody answered him. The theater doors opened and they swarmed in, forgetting him.

The woman with the coffee cart called him over. She gave Jim a mug of coffee to warm him up.

"Seen you skipping," she said. "How's that friend of yours? He still bad?"

Jim nodded. He wished he could carry the mug of coffee to Shrimps, but he knew it wouldn't do any good. Jim gulped the coffee down. "I'm looking for a doctor for him. Don't know one, do you? One that won't charge. I could do jobs for him."

She frowned. "There is a doctor of some sort, not far from here. But I've never heard of him doing any doctoring, like. Barnie something, they call him. The little kids next door to me go to his school."

"School? I don't want anything to do with school." Jim remembered the schoolroom at the workhouse— the lofty room, the boys quiet and afraid at their desks, the pacing schoolmaster.

"The Ragged School. Ain't you heard of it?" the woman went on. She stopped to serve someone pickled eggs and coffee. "All I know is it's somewhere kids go when they don't have money to pay for school. They do a lot of praying."

Again Jim remembered the schoolroom with the painted arches: God is good, God is holy, God is just, God is love. He could hear again the thin chanting of the boys' voices as they recited it every day.

"No," he said, shaking his head. "I wouldn't go there, missus. Never."

"Suit yourself," she said. "He's the only doctor I know of."

But during that night, Shrimps grew worse. He was hot and feverish, and weak though he was, he coughed all the time. Jim put his hand under his friend's head to prop him up. He pulled away the straw to push some fresh under, and saw that it was spotted with blood.

25

The Ragged School

Next morning, early, he waited for the coffee woman to bring her cart. When he saw her dragging it up through the mud, he ran to meet her.

"He's worse," he panted. "Can you come to him?"

"I can't leave my stall," she told him. "If I don't give breakfast to the early workers, I've lost my best trade."

"If you tell me where that school is, I'll go there."

"It's round about. Over there somewhere. Somewhere around Ernest Street." The woman waved her arm vaguely. She was sorry enough for the boy, but there were plenty more where he came from. Skinny, helpless sparrows. The streets were full of them. If she helped one, the rest'd be around for help. She had her own children to feed, and the rent to pay, or they'd all be out in the streets. All in the same state as Jim. It didn't bear thinking about. She had to keep going.

Jim ran off. Some of the street boys shouted after him, "How's Shrimps?" but Jim didn't even bother to tell them. No child could help Shrimps now.

"Know where the Ragged School is?" he asked one of them, a crippled boy called Davey, who was older than most of them. Davey shook his head.

"I've heard of it," he said. "There was a man with a donkey used to come around wanting boys to go to his school. We used to chuck tomatoes at him, though. School!" He spat out of the corner of his mouth. "Don't trust them places, I don't."

Jim managed to coax some milk from a dairywoman, and he ran back to Shrimps with it, moistening the boy's lips. His hair was dark with sweat, but he was cold.

"Please let them take you to the hospital, Shrimps," he said, but Shrimps shook his head.

"I'm all right here. Proper little palace, this crate."

Davey and some of the younger boys came to see Shrimps, and Jim left him to them and went off again. At last, when it was nearly dark, he came across a group of children—brothers and sisters they must have been, they were so alike. They were coming up a back alley-way together, and some of them were clutching slates. They were dressed in rags, but they obviously had a home to go to.

"Have you been to the Ragged School?" Jim asked them.

One of them nodded.

"Is there a doctor there?"

The children looked at one another. "That Barnie bloke said he was a doctor, didn't he?"

"That's right. Only 'e don't give us medicine, 'e gives us hymns!"

One of the children started singing, and the others giggled.

"Where is it?"

The older child ran back with Jim and pointed out a long, shedlike building. "There it is," he said. "And there's that Barnie bloke, just coming out now."

Jim raced down the street. The man locked the door of the shed and began to move quickly in the other direction.

"Dr. Barnie!" Jim shouted out, but his voice was drowned out by the rumble of carriage wheels. He pressed himself against the wall to let the carriage pass. The doctor raised his hand as the carriage approached, and the driver reined in his horse. Jim started running again. "Doctor!" he shouted.

But the man hadn't heard him. He climbed up into the carriage and was away before Jim reached it. Mud spattered up into Jim's face.

When he got back to the crates behind the market, the other boys had gone. Someone had placed a small candle in a bowl, and its soft light was some kind of comfort in the dark. Jim crawled in beside Shrimps.

"It's going to be all right now," he whispered. "I've found a doctor, and he's coming to see you tomorrow."

But even as he spoke, the words were like stones in his throat. He reached out and felt for the boy's hand. It was cold.

26

Good-bye, Bruvver

Old Samuel, the night watchman, took Shrimps's body into his hut. He set candles around it, and as the street boys heard of his death, they came to have a look at him. They came in groups and stood in a huddle in the doorway, not daring to come in, and soon ran off again.

Jim sat with his head in his hands all day. Samuel shook him by his shoulder.

"Reckon you'll have to go, Skippin' Jim," he told him. "They'll be bringing the pauper's cart for Shrimps here soon, an' if they sees you here, you knows where they'll take you."

Jim didn't care. He almost felt it would be good to be back in the workhouse. He would see Joseph again, and Tip. His life would be ordered and regular; there'd be food at mealtimes and sleep at bedtimes. He wouldn't have to run away from anyone, or hide, or steal food. But then he thought of the mad people wailing, and the runaway boys in their cage; the chil-

dren crying in the night, the long, echoing, dark corridors, and the sound of keys turning in locks. Shrimps
had died rather than go back there. Well. So would he.

Samuel went out to call six o'clock at the street
corners. Jim took a last look around the quiet hut with
its dim candles, and at the figure wrapped in a sack. He
took his boots out of his pockets. They were in shreds.

"Bye, bruvver," he said. He put the boots next to the
sack and slipped away.

He had no idea where to go now. He couldn't live
in the crates again, not without Shrimps. He shivered
in a shop doorway until he saw policemen coming,
then darted across the road. It was easy to hide in the
darkness between the lamps, but he couldn't stay there
all night. It was too cold to stand still, and too muddy
to sit down.

For the first time, he wondered where all the other
street boys slept. He remembered what one of the boys
had said: "He ain't got the strength to climb up with
us, so we brought him here."

Climb? Jim thought. Climb where?

He wandered around the back of the crates, around
behind the market stalls. Nothing. Nothing to see. Yet
he thought he could hear a slight burst of chattering,
like the whistlings of starlings. He stood still. The
sound was coming from over his head. Then he heard
a slight scuffing. He glanced around. No one in sight.
He ran to the support wall of the market and heaved
himself up, hand over fist, and at last hauled himself
onto the roof. He stood up slowly, gazing across at

the looped tarpaulin. Everywhere he looked there were black bundles, like little heaps of rags, but as he stood still and let his eyes grow used to the new darkness, he could see that those bundles were boys, huddled up for the night on their rooftop home.

27

Barnie

There was no comfort there. At night the wind seemed to crack around the boys like a whip. When it rained they would wake up soaked to the skin, and it would be days before they dried off, sometimes. Jim used to lie huddled up, looking at the stars and listening to the boys' breathing. "This ain't home," he said to himself.

When morning came with its sooty mist, the boys would roll down the wall to be on the alert before the police were about, trying to earn a few pennies to buy themselves a night in a lodging house. They ate what they could, grabbing a bit of cheese here or a crust of pie there, and if they were caught they were hauled off before a magistrate and sent to the workhouse. Jim wasn't as fast as the other boys because of his bad leg, and the only job he could think of doing was skipping for the theater queues, which made a few people smile, anyway. The other boys worked in gangs when they were stealing, passing the scarf or purse from one to the other so rapidly that it was impossible to tell what was happening. To Jim they were like a big family helping one another. But he wasn't one of them. They tended to leave him on his own.

One day, when he woke up drenched to the skin again, coughing and shaking with cold, he knew he'd had enough.

"If you go on like this, Jim, you'll be where Shrimps is," he told himself. "There must be summat else, bruvver."

It was then that he remembered the Ragged School. He thought of the long shed that the school was held in.

Somewhere to keep warm, he thought. And that Barnie bloke looked all right. He won't hit you, he won't.

He decided to give it a try, just for a day. He wandered around until he found the shed again. Children were crowding around the door when he arrived, waiting to be let in. The shed was a big room with boards laid on top of soil for a floor. The walls and rafters had been painted a dingy white, and there were bars across the windows. There was a good fire burning in a grate. Jim sidled up to it. There must have been over a hundred children there. They sat in rows, but there were so many of them that some of them were on the floor.

Jim gazed around him, listening to their chatter, and to the way it faded down when the teacher stood up to talk to them in his gentle, lilting voice. He was a tall, slim man with straight brown hair and fluffy side-whiskers and spectacles. Jim recognized him straight-away as the man Lame Betsy had taken him to listen to in the back alley. He remembered shouting out at him, and how some of the boys had chucked mud balls at him. And he remembered the man's sad eyes. He ducked his head down, worried now in case he would be recognized and thrown out into the cold.

Yet he could see that the children weren't afraid of the man. They didn't flinch away from him as if they expected him to hit them at any minute. They called him Teacher, and they seemed to be happy to do what-ever he told them, though they murmured and giggled among themselves as if they couldn't concentrate for very long. The teacher man didn't seem to mind. Occa-sionally he looked at Jim, but always Jim put his head down or glanced quickly away.

At the end of the day the man asked all the children to stand up and pray with him, and again Jim looked away. He was the only child still sitting, but the man didn't seem to mind. They finished off the day with a hymn, which all the children yelled out cheerfully be-fore they were sent off home.

Still Jim sat by the fire, hoping not to be noticed. The Barnie man finished straightening up the benches and wiping the board, and at last he came over to Jim. Jim clenched his hands together, staring down at them, ready to run if the man hit him. But he didn't. Instead, he sat down next to Jim and warmed his hands by the fire.

"It's time for me to blow the lights out," he said in his soft voice.

Jim didn't move.

"Come on, my lad," the Barnie man said. "It's time to go home now."

Jim clenched and unclenched his fists. The gentleness in the man's voice made his throat ache.

The man stood up. "Come on now. You'd better go home at once."

Jim tried to make his voice come. "Please, sir. Let me stay."

"Stay?" The man stared down at him. "What for? I'm going to put the lights out and lock the door. It's quite time for a young boy like you to go home and get to bed. What do you want to stay for?"

"Please, sir," said Jim, not looking at the man, but at the flames in the fire, which made his eyes smart and blur.

"You ought to go home at once," Barnie insisted. "Your mother will know the other boys have gone. She'll wonder what kept you so late."

"I ain't got no mother."

"Your father, then."

"I ain't got no father."

Barnie was getting impatient, Jim could see that. It was almost as if he didn't believe him. "Where are your friends, then? Where do you live?"

"Ain't got no friends. Don't live nowhere."

Barnie stared at him. He walked away from the fire and back to it again, then went to the desk. He sat down in his chair and stayed with his fingers drumming across the flat of the desktop, like the patter of rain on a roof. Jim wondered if he was angry with him.

"It's the truth, sir," he said anxiously. "I ain't telling you no lies." He spoke in the whiny voice the other street boys used to adults.

"Tell me," the man said at last. "How many boys are there like you? Sleeping out in the streets?"

"Heaps," said Jim. "More than I can count."

It was Barnie's turn now to stare into the fire, as if there were secrets in its flames, or answers to great puzzles. He was as still and quiet as if he had gone to sleep, and Jim kept still, too, afraid to break into the man's thinking. The only sound was the spitting of the logs, and outside, the bleak voice of the wind.

"Now," the man said, very slowly, like someone creeping up on a bird in case he frightened it away, "if I am willing to give you a hot meal and a place to sleep in, will you take me to where some of these other boys are?"

Jim looked sideways at him. "You wouldn't tell the police?"

"No," said Barnie. "I wouldn't tell the police."

"All right," said Jim. "I'll take you."

It was some time later that they arrived at the high wall of the market. Jim stopped, afraid again. What if Barnie did tell the police about them, and sent all the boys to the workhouse? But if he didn't show Barnie, he wouldn't get the hot meal and the shelter to sleep in. He didn't know what to do. Barnie seemed to understand and just stood waiting and watching while Jim glanced from side to side, afraid to be seen by anyone in the man's company.

Jim had almost made up his mind to run away and leave him standing there when the man said, "What's your name?"

"Jim, sir." Out it came, and it sounded such a special thing. That's it now, Jim thought to himself. That's the last thing I've got, and I've just give it away.

"Where are they, Jim?"

"Up there, sir." Jim pointed to the roof of the market shed.

"There? And how am I to get up there?"

"I'll show you." Jim made light work of it. There were well-worn marks on the bricks where the mortar had fallen or been picked away. Jim shinned up quickly and then leaned over the edge, holding down a stick. Barnie grabbed it and heaved himself up, then stood shakily, brushing his clothes and his grazed hands. He held up his lantern.

And there, all around him, lay the boys, curled up in their rags of clothes, sleeping like dogs.

And this man, Barnie—well, I never seen a grown-up look so sad, and that's the truth. He just looked and looked, as if he couldn't believe his eyes. I was shivering next to him, and I thought he was never going to move or stop looking. I thought he was going to stay there all night.

"So this is where you live, is it, Jim?" he asked me.

"Yes," I said, and I felt sad for him then, because he looked as if he felt as if it was all his fault. Know what I mean?

And then he said, "Well, how about that meal I promised you?" and that cheered me up, because I thought he'd forgotten all about that. He started to climb down the wall, skidding a bit because he had boots on, and it's not so easy if you're not in bare feet. He took me to a house and gave me a meal and let me have a hot bath. And do you know what he said? He said, "I'm going to give you a home, Jim."

I went back with him next day to the rooftop, and I told the other boys about him. It wasn't long before they all decided to come with me. There's so many boys wanting homes now that he's asking rich people for money to open another house for them. That's why he wanted to know my story, see?

It's like having lots of brothers, living here. We all sleep in a big upstairs room with a roaring fire and swingy hammocks hanging from the ceiling. We get plenty to eat.

Barnie tells us about God a lot and he's kind to us. He gets us jobs to do like chopping wood and we get paid, fair and square, and then we pay him for our meals.

And there's nothing to keep us here. Can't believe that, I can't. No bars on the windows or locks on the doors. No beatings. I could run away tomorrow if I wanted to.

But I don't, see? I'm Jim Jarvis, I am. And this is my home.

Author's Note

Jim Jarvis was a real boy, but not very much is known about him. I've tried to imagine what his life was like up to the time when he met a man called Dr. Barnardo in about 1866.

Thomas John Barnardo was born in Ireland in 1845. He came to London to study medicine but never qualified, though he liked to be known as Dr. Barnardo. He was eager to become a missionary in China but soon decided that his real mission was to help the poor children in the streets of London. First he opened up Ragged Schools in the 1860s, and then he opened up his first home for destitute children, a Cottage Home, in Stepney, London, in 1867. Barnardo was not a wealthy man himself but raised money for the homes by writing pamphlets about the orphans he came across. He often said that meeting Jim Jarvis was what made him aware of the real plight of destitute children in London.

Jim did run away from a workhouse after his mother

died, and was helped by a woman who sold whelks and shrimps. He lived for a time on a coal lighter with a man and dog and was treated very cruelly. After he ran away from them, he lived in the streets and slept on the rooftops until he went to one of Dr. Barnardo's Ragged School classes and asked him for help.

Shrimps is based on Jack Somers, also known as Carrots, who actually came to Dr. Barnardo's notice a little later. In real life Carrots died of starvation in a crate before Barnardo could give him a home. His tragic story also greatly influenced Dr. Barnardo, who put a notice on the doors of the Cottage Homes—NO DESTITUTE BOY EVER REFUSED ADMISSION.

Soon Barnardo began to open homes for girls, too. He died in 1905, but his work became known throughout the world, and many of his homes survived. The charity, now called Barnardo's, still exists today to help young people in all kinds of ways.

Some of the books I used for background research:
Ackroyd, *Dickens*
Chesney, *The Victorian Underworld*
Dickens (ed.), *All the Year Round* (journals)
Hibbert, *The Making of Charles Dickens*
Mayhew, *London Labour and the London Poor*
Midwinter, *Victorian Social Reform*
Pyke, *Human Documents of the Age of the Forsythes*
Seaman, *Life in Victorian London*